Mudsills & Mooncussers

IRIS CHACON

ISBN: 1519779259
ISBN-13: 978-1519779250

DEDICATION

To Mr. Wonderful, who provided all the time, travel, and resources for researching and writing this novel, and who is God's great undeserved blessing upon my life.

ACKNOWLEDGMENTS

Many thanks to the librarians at the Monroe County Public Library on Key West, especially those in the Florida/local history room who allowed me to spend hours reading the diaries of 19th-century Key West residents.

Thanks also to the booksellers of Key West who helped me to find and obtain hard-to-find books by and about the Conchs.

Finally, heartfelt thanks to those brave beta readers who accepted the challenge of reading the manuscript – my father most of all.

CONTENTS

PROLOGUE

In 1860, the small population of a two- by four-mile island called Key West, southern tip of the United States, had grown wealthy upon the wreckage of ships. The noble citizens of Key West often rescued passengers and crews when tall-masted wooden ships were forced by storms onto the shallow, knife-edged coral reefs lining the Gulf Stream waters called the Florida Straits. Maritime law stated that the first boat captain to hail the foundering vessel earned the right to salvage and sell whatever could be taken off the wreck before the sea claimed it.

Less noble citizens had been known to build fires on nearby islands north of the official Key West lighthouse. Such a false light could cause helmsmen to turn toward the shore miles before it was safe to do so, driving their doomed ship onto the reefs and into the hands of the waiting wreckers. Black, moonless nights worked best for luring unwary mariners onto the rocks. For that reason, these dishonest ship wreckers were known as "mooncussers." In the worst cases, mooncussers had been known to kill—or perhaps merely fail to rescue—both passengers and sailors. Dead men tell no tales.

The wrecking business was lucrative—and sometimes even honest—and by the 1850s had made Key West the richest town per capita in Florida. Of course, there were few towns in the state at that time. Citizens of Key West did their shopping in Mobile, Alabama, or Charleston, South Carolina. The nearest Florida ports of any significance were Tampa and St. Augustine. At the mouth of the Miami River was a small trading post at meager Fort Dallas, but the city of Miami would not be born until the century after the War Between the States.

The American Civil War played out in microcosm on the tiny island of Key West. Located just 90 miles north of Havana, Cuba, Key West was a community of staunch southerners—indeed, they considered themselves the southernmost of the southerners. The cay was too small for even one plantation and housed few slaves. Still, as a matter of pure geography, no one was more southern than the "Conchs" of Key West.

That's why it was so ironic, and more than a little vexing, that a small battalion of Northern soldiers managed to march out of their barracks one night and steal across the island and into its only significant military installation: the mostly-completed Fort Zachary Taylor. Thus it was that, when the metaphorical smoke cleared over Fort Sumter, South Carolina, and war began in earnest, the southern citizens of Key West found their city occupied by Yankee soldiers without a shot having been fired.

Key West was to remain in Union hands throughout the war. But since nobody had the prescience to know that fact ahead of time, the North and South waged war in their own unique way on the miniscule island at the bottom of the North American map.

The war on Key West began quietly at twilight on January 13, 1861. The sun's fiery ball sank into the blue-green Gulf of Mexico at the edge of the world. Clouds bled pink and purple. Bird shadows fled to their roosts across the red-orange orb or splashed into the limitless sea, spearing a last-minute meal and carrying it away.

While the city of Key West slept, a small group of Yankee soldiers slogged through the dead of night, avoiding the main part of town, and surreptitiously took up occupancy in an unfinished brick fort on the southern tip of the southernmost island of the United States. It was Fort Zachary Taylor, and the secessionist citizens of Key West had been actively planning to move into it in the immediate future.

Wooden sailing ships crowded the harbor. Tift's Ice House, the Custom House, and various warehouses squatted on the shoreline. Bahama-style homes lined the wide dirt streets with names like Whitehead and Duval that ran from water to water, across the small island.

Key West was the most strategic point in the Confederacy, covering access from the Atlantic Ocean and Caribbean Sea to the Gulf of Mexico and the Confederate harbor cities from Texas to Florida. This small band of Union soldiers, fearing attack at any time by the Key Westers who had been thwarted in the taking of Fort Jefferson, would hold Key West for the Union until reinforcements could arrive. They had four months' provisions and 70,000 gallons of fresh water—for which the only source on Key West was rainwater.

When April arrived, and with it the anticipated Union reinforcements, that first puny band of soldiers breathed a sigh of relief. After four tense, exhausting months as minority representatives of the United States of America, surrounded by Confederate citizens, the Yankees' numbers had finally increased. Their position in the fort was secure. They thought the worst was over, the hard work was done. Of course, they were wrong.

CHAPTER 1

1862

Sergeant Jules Pfifer, a career Army man, marched his patrol briskly through the evening heat toward a tall wooden house on the corner of Whitehead Street and Duval Street. Atop the house was perched a square cupola surrounded by the sailor-carved balustrades called gingerbread. These porches, just large enough for one or two persons to stand and observe the sea from the rooftop, were known as widows' walks. From this particular widow's walk an illegal Confederate flag flaunted its red stars and bars against the clear Key West sky.

The soldiers in Union blue marched smartly through the gate in the white picket fence, up the front steps, and in at the front door—which opened before them as if by magic.

"Evenin', Miz Lowe," Sergeant Pfifer said, without breaking stride, to the woman who had opened the door.

"Evenin', Sergeant," the lady of the house answered, unperturbed.

On the Lowe house roof, the stars and bars were whipped from their post; they disappeared from sight just as the soldiers, clomping and puffing and sweat-stained, arrived atop the stairway. Pfifer and another man crowded onto the widow's walk. Consternation wrinkled the soldiers' faces when they found no Confederate flag, only 17-year-old Caroline Lowe, smiling sweetly.

...

In the twilight, the three-story brick trapezoid of Fort Zachary Taylor loomed castle-like over the sea waves. It stood on its own 63-acre shoal, connected to the island of Key West by a narrow 1000-foot causeway. The fort had taken 21 years to build and was plagued by constant shortages of men and material as well as outbreaks of deadly yellow fever.

Yankee sentries paced between the black silhouettes of cannon pointed seaward. Firefly lights of campfires and lanterns sparkled on the parade ground and among the Sibley tents huddled on shore at the base of the causeway.

Midway between the fort and Caroline Lowe's flagpole, on the tin roof of a three-story wooden house, behind the gingerbread railing of another widow's walk, two athletic, handsome youngsters stood close together, blown by the wind. Twenty-year-old Richard scanned the sea with a spyglass. Joe, an inch shorter than Richard, kept one hand atop a floppy hat the wind wanted to steal.

Richard found something interesting to the east. He handed over the spyglass and pointed Joe toward the same point on the horizon. Joe searched, then zeroed in.

"Some rascal's laid a false light over on Boca Chica," Richard said, referring to the smaller island just northeast of Key West. "Come on!"

They tucked the spyglass into a hollow rail of the widow's walk and hastened down the stairs.

...

On neighboring Boca Chica island, night blanketed the beach. A hunched figure tossed a branch onto a blazing bonfire then slunk away into the darkness. Pine pitch popped and crackled in the fire, adding its sweet aroma to the tang of the salty breeze coming off the sea.

...

Inside a warehouse on Tift's Wharf, all shapes and sizes of kegs, boxes, and wooden crates towered in jagged heaps. Sickly yellow light from a sailor's lantern sent quivering shadows across the stacks. A spindly boy of 15, Joseph Porter, kept watch through a crack in the door.

On the floor a dozen teenaged boys hunkered down, whispering. Richard sneaked in from the rear of the building to join them. Behind him, out of the light and keeping quiet, came Joe.

Porter hissed, "Mudsills comin'!"

The whispered buzz of conversation halted.

Someone doused the light. Bodies thumped to the floor as the boys took cover.

Outside, footsteps ground into the gravelly dirt of the street. Four Yankee soldiers, the source of the boys' concern, completed a weary circuit of the dark dockside buildings. They were Pennsylvania farm boys not much older than the Key West boys hiding inside.

The southern boys would have been surprised to know that the Yankees in the street were not technically "mudsills," that was the name given to northern factory workers who lived crowded together in dirt-floored shacks along muddy streets. Still, the word was applied to all the Yankee enemies, just as the northern boys would have called Key West residents "mooncussers," as if they all were pirates.

Native born citizens of Key West referred to themselves as Conchs, a term dating back to the 1780s immigration of British Loyalists from the Bahamas. A large shellfish called a conch was plentiful in the local waters and became a staple of the pioneers' diet.

On Tift's Wharf one of the Pennsylvania soldiers said something in Dutch-German, and the others murmured agreement. They sounded homesick. One slapped a mosquito on his neck then turned up his collar, grumbling.

In front of the warehouse the soldiers stopped beside a barrel set to catch rainwater running off the tin roof during storms. They loosened their woolen tunics and dipped their handkerchiefs into the water, laving themselves, trying in vain to ease the steamy agony of tropical heat.

Inside, the wide-eyed Conch boys held their breath, listening to the sounds from the water barrel outside. Joseph Porter trembled, perspired, and stared cross-eyed at a gigantic mosquito making itself at home on the end of his nose. He tried to raise one hand quietly to chase the brute away, but his elbow nudged a crate of bottles. Glass tinkled. The boys froze.

Outside, a soldier started at the sound and snatched up his weapon. *"Vas ist das?"*

The other soldiers were less concerned. They were hot, tired, and not looking for trouble.

"Rats," one said. "These pirate ships are full of them. Let's go back to the ice house. It's cooler."

The sweat-covered Conch boys heard the receding footsteps of the Yankees. Long, sweltering seconds later, Porter crept to his crack in the door and risked a peek. "It's all right. They're gone."

Red-haired William Sawyer lit the lantern.

A bigger boy, Marcus Oliveri, stepped forward and cuffed Porter smartly. "Porter, you imbecile!"

"Here now, Marcus!" said William. "He didn't mean to."

Oliveri returned to his place in the circle of boys forming around the lantern. "I don't fancy getting arrested or maybe shot because Porter can't abide getting mosquito bit for his country!"

"I'm sorry," said Porter. "It was an accident."

"Let's just forget it," urged William. "Let's finish up and get out of here before they come back. Now, the English schooner leaves for Nassau tomorrow morning. Richard and Marcus and Alfred and me will be on it. The rest of you know what to do to cover for us."

An older boy with a thick Bahamian accent, Alfred Lowe, shook his finger under the nose of a friend. "And you, Bogy Sands, stay away from my sister while I'm gone, you hear me?"

Richard looked surprised. He thought he and Caroline Lowe had an unspoken agreement. "Caroline? Bogy!"

"You ain't engaged to her, Thibodeaux," said Bogy.

William Sawyer's hair flashed the same fiery color as the lamplight when he reached across the circle to separate Richard and Bogy. "That's enough of that! Let's not be fighting each other. God willing, we'll all be soldiers of the Seventh Florida Regiment within the year. Any questions?"

All around the circle the boys murmured in the negative.

"Let's get home then, and be ready when the call comes," William said.

The boys scrambled away. Joe and Richard were the last to leave, watching for Yankee patrols while the others sneaked out.

Joe complained, "I'll probably break my neck walking around in your boots. You got such big feet, Wretched! I had to stuff the toes with rags."

"You just keep that hat on and stay out of Papa's way. You'll do fine," Richard replied.

As they moved to leave the warehouse, Richard put an arm around Joe's shoulders and gave an encouraging squeeze.

...

In the Florida Straits between Key West and Cuba, just before dawn, two lithe, black fishermen reacted to the flare of a distress signal that arced upward in the eastern sky. One fisherman reached into the bilge of his craft and produced the empty pink-and-white spiraling shell of that large mollusk called a conch. He lifted the trumpet-size conch shell to his lips and blew a loud, hooting blast.

Seconds later on Tift's Wharf, a lookout in a wooden tower reacted to the distant conch horn, scanned the eastern horizon with a spyglass for barely an instant, then clanged the wreckers' bell and shouted to wake the whole island.

"Wreck asho-o-o-re! Wreck asho-o-o-re!"

Men of all sizes came running from every direction. Black men and white, old and young, in jerseys and loose short pants, they raced through the streets of Key West to the Jamaica sloops moored in the harbor. Every shopkeeper (save one, William Curry) left his store, every clergyman his church, every able-bodied homeowner his house. Quickly it became apparent that nearly every man in Key West, whatever else he might be, was a wrecker.

Men shouted, the bell clanged, the distant conch horn trumpeted. The race was on. Yankee soldiers, standing on the street corner, did well not to be trampled in the rush.

At Fort Taylor, blue-clad soldiers on the roof of the fort took note of the wreck and watched closely the activity in the harbor, ready to take action if necessary.

Aboard the moored schooner *Lady Alyce*, white-bearded, patriarchal Captain Elias Thibodeaux, regal in his double-breasted jacket, surveyed the scene with hawk's eyes. The *Lady Alyce,* at 50 feet and 136 tons, was a sleek topsail schooner with well-greased masts, coiled lines, and shining brightwork. She looked like she could outsail anything.

"Mister Simmons," the captain shouted.

The mate, Cataline Simmons, was a black Bahamian with the muscles and instincts of an experienced sailor and the accent of an Oxford professor. "Aye, sir!"

Thibodeau's eyes searched the wharf again, but it was no use. What he sought was not there. "Hoist the mains'l," he commanded.

Cataline, too, looked with concern at the wharf before executing the order.

"Today, Simmons!" bellowed the captain. "We'll leave him if we have to, but I will be first to bespeak that wreck!"

Cataline leapt into action, gesturing to four crewmen—three white, one black—who waited poised at their stations. "Aye, sir! Hoist the mains'l."

The three white crewmen set about their tasks quickly, skillfully. The small, wiry black man, Stepney

Austin, hesitated. If Thibodeaux was king here, and he undoubtedly was, then Stepney Austin was the court jester. Monkeylike in his movements and Cockney in his speech, he could be the bane of Simmons' existence if he were not so brave and loyal.

"Cast off the docklines," said the captain.

Cataline threw Stepney a look. Stepney moved as if he had been waiting for just such an order.

The sail was filling; other boats were getting underway. Stepney cast off the bow lines and moved deliberately toward the stern, watching the wharf as did Cataline. Thibodeaux turned away and looked seaward, giving up on finding what he sought upon the wharf.

Then Joe, baggy in Richard's clothing and unsteady in Richard's boots, appeared at the far side of the wharf, running toward the *Lady Alyce.*

Stepney cried, "There he is!"

Thibodeaux did not look. "Cast off!"

Cataline lifted a cargo block hanging from the rigging nearby and, as he spoke, swung the block like a great pendulum out over the wharf. "Casting off. Aye, aye, sir."

Stepney was forced to comply, but it was in slow motion that he cast off the stern line.

Joe ran desperately to close the gap of several yards between Richard's reluctant boots and the departing schooner. When the cargo block swung toward Joe, Joe took full advantage of it by grabbing it and hanging on for dear life.

Stepney chanted, "Come on, come on!"

Joe's forward motion combined with the pendulum swing of the block to carry Joe, like a trapeze artist, across the chasm now yawning between schooner and wharf. Joe landed more-or-less flatfooted on the deck behind Captain Thibodeaux. Richard's floppy hat tumbled from Joe's head, followed by a cascade of unruly curls that reached halfway down her back.

CHAPTER 2

Stepney Austin lurched forward and opened his mouth, only to find Cataline Simmons's hand clapped across his face. Cataline gestured with a sidewise tilt of his head to the schooner across the harbor—the one flying the English flag—then glared disapproval at Joe and the errant hat.

Joe grabbed the hat, stuffed the telltale curls into it, and replaced it on her head.

Thibodeaux still did not look around. "Good morning, Richard. So good of you to join us. Now get aloft and find me that wreck."

"Aye, sir!" said Joe and climbed for the top of the mast. The other crewmen tackled their duties with renewed relish. Cataline and Stepney exchanged a look. The wrecking fleet departed, leaving behind the English schooner, with four young stow-aways on board, across the harbor.

...

On Pelican Shoal, near the edge of the Gulf

Stream's warm current, the *St. Gertrude,* a 200-foot merchantman, sat at an odd angle, jarring, creaking, and shuddering. Waves whapped her sides and wind jangled her rigging. She had wedged her keel firmly aground. A dozen anxious crewmen lined the *St. Gertrude's* rail, watching the *Lady Alyce* approach, trailed by other wrecking sloops—though none within 300 yards of her.

It appeared that a young boy in floppy hat and baggy clothes stood at the helm of the *Lady Alyce.* The white-bearded, red-coated captain was an imposing figure as he stepped into the bow and hailed the grounded merchantman. "Ahoy, *St. Gertrude!*"

Aaron Matthews, a tall, well-built man in a brocade jacket, returned a lusty shout from the bridge of the merchantman. "Ahoy, yourself! Can we assist you?"

Thibodeaux smiled at the younger man's audacity. "Could you stand to lighten your load a bit?"

"Have you come to rob me, then?" replied Matthews.

"Naw! Naw, no need for that. We'll just bide here 'til the next tide breaks you up and take what's left. Or we could pull you off, see you safe into Key West, and let the admiralty court decide who gets what."

The young captain of the *St. Gertrude* was considering his options when his arm was taken by a beautiful woman who came up behind him—an antebellum china doll, from the taffeta hoop skirt to the shiny hair piled high on her head, showing off her dainty dangling earrings. This was Lila Dauthier.

"You're not seriously thinking of allowing those ... those *mooncussers* to come aboard, are you, Aaron?" Lila simpered.

"I was, yes."

"But, sweetheart! Everyone knows they're no better than pirates. Vultures. They cause ships to wreck just so they can loot them."

Aaron fondled her earring and teased her with a smile. "They may have played a trick or two in their time, Lila my dove, but I can hardly blame them for this one, since I myself was at the helm. Someone must have distracted me."

Aaron had amused himself with Lila in the past, and they had renewed their acquaintance aboard the *St. Gertrude* in recent days, but in truth he found her shallow and annoying, regardless of her obvious physical charms. He was enough of a cad to use the ladies and discard them casually. He was enough of a gentleman that his paramours never felt his disinterest, never perceived him disrespectful. In every instance, his women felt he had been prevented from continuing their pleasant liaison by circumstances beyond his control. There was a war on, naturally.

Aboard the *Lady Alyce*, Captain Thibodeaux knew the other sloops were drawing closer, but his position as master of this wreck was secure. He took in the situation with a shrewd look and shouted to the stranded vessel, "*St. Gertrude!* Have we permission to come aboard?"

Lila gave Aaron her most persuasive pleading look, but his smile told her she had lost this argument.

"Very well," she said. "I shall be in my cabin—securing my valuables."

Aaron watched her leave the bridge, her gait calculated to keep his attention. Suddenly he was in an expansive mood. He called over the rail, "Come aboard, my friends! Do your worst!"

"On the contrary, sir," Thibodeaux shouted. "We shall, as always, do our best!"

Thibodeaux gestured to his crewmen, who moved to carry out his unspoken order. Joe, at the helm, worked the *Lady Alyce* close alongside the *St. Gertrude,* where crewmen tied her up.

While Joe concentrated on this maneuver, Captain Thibodeaux took a seat near the helm, and lit his pipe. He spoke for Joe's ears alone.

"Richard never saw the day he could make six knots through Dry Rocks in a wind like we had today. I don't know what shenanigans you two are about, Josephine Marie, but if you're fool enough to take Richard's place, I'll expect you to keep your hat on and carry Richard's share of the load. Is that clear?"

Joe swallowed hard. "Aye, aye, sir. Clear as a bell."

A trace of a smile showed behind Thibodeaux's beard and pipe as he rose to step away. "Your mama'll kill you when you get home, I reckon. Don't suppose you'd tell me where Richard has taken himself off to? Courting Caroline Lowe, maybe?"

"I don't know exactly where he is this minute," Joe answered truthfully.

...

Miles away, in the Gulf Stream, the English schooner had left Key West harbor behind and was making excellent headway under full sail toward the Bahamas. Aboard were four Conch boys on their way to join the Confederate Army.

...

On the streets of Key West, a patrol of Yankee soldiers made its way under the glaring mid-day sun toward Tift's Wharf. Something atop one of the houses on Duval Street caught Sergeant Pfifer's eye. "Shades of 'Barbara Frietchie,' she's at it again!" the sergeant cried. "Come on!"

A gray-haired lady and her plumpish daughter sat on the wide front porch of the Lowe house, plying their knitting needles. The sergeant and his men trooped through the front gate, strode up the walk, climbed the porch steps, and proceeded directly to the front door. A black house servant, waiting inside the door, swung it open just before they could crash into it. The ladies on the porch took no notice of the procession.

"Mornin', Miz Lowe. Miz Euphemie," mumbled the sergeant in passing.

On the Lowe house rooftop, feisty Caroline

Lowe stood next to an improvised flagpole wherefrom waved her homemade Confederate flag. She watched the soldiers disappear through the front door below her, headed her way. She began taking down the flag with practiced speed.

The sergeant led his men, huffing and puffing in their woolen blue jackets, up the interior stairs to the roof. "Today's the day, Miss Caroline," he muttered. "Today we've got you."

Sergeant Pfifer and his men emerged onto the widow's walk to find Caroline waving to an admiring Bogy Sands, who watched from the street below. No flag—and no place to hide a flag—anywhere in sight.

The sergeant looked at Caroline's long, full skirt, but abandoned that idea for numerous reasons. He looked over the widow's walk railing on all four sides. Nothing. He looked at empty-handed Bogy Sands in the street below. He gave up. He turned back and growled at his men in frustration, "Search the house!"

The men piled back downstairs, mumbling. One said, "We searched the house yesterday."

"We'll search it again today and every day until we find that blasted pennant! Good day, Miss Caroline."

The lady answered with a thick 'Brilander British accent, "Always a pleasure, Sergeant."

...

It was nearly dusk in Key West harbor when the wrecking fleet returned, crowding the anchorage. All around, boats were made fast, and weary sailors headed homeward on foot.

Joe left the *Lady Alyce* and was greeted on shore by Joseph Porter. Together they turned and looked at the empty mooring where the English schooner had been that morning.

"They made it, Joe!" said Porter. "They got away clean."

"Yeah," she said. "Now comes the hard part."

"Fightin' the Yankees!"

"Telling my mother."

CHAPTER 3

Minutes later, in the dusk at Fort Zachary Taylor, Colonel T.H. Good stood on the ramparts, 50 feet above Key West harbor and the Gulf of Mexico, observing the activities on Tift's Wharf through his spyglass. A noise attracted Colonel Good's attention—someone climbing the steps from the parade ground to the shadows behind him. The colonel did not turn to look at the newcomer.

"Matheson?" the colonel ventured.

"Matthews, sir," answered a deep voice from the shadows.

Colonel Good continued his observations, throwing his words over his shoulder. "Matthews, then. If I may say so, Lieutenant, you chose the devil's own way to get here. But for your encounter with Pelican Shoal, I might have had to arrest you for a blockade runner. A lot of help you'd be to me sitting in jail at Fort Jefferson."

"You would've had to catch me first." The silence lingered almost too long before Aaron added,

"Sir."

Colonel Good lowered his spyglass and delivered an affectionate pat to a massive black cannon pointing toward the sea. "Lieutenant, if I thought there was a ghost of a chance we wouldn't catch you, I'd have blown you out of the water. And if I didn't, the Union Navy's blockade ships would. And if they didn't, the guns at Fort Jefferson would. We are the gateposts to the Gulf, Lieutenant. Nobody gets into our yard without being seen by one or the other of us."

"May I beg the colonel's indulgence to continue this audience in the colonel's office?" asked Aaron.

"You may not. This wind keeps the infernal mosquitos at bay, and I am partial to these sunsets."

The western sky glowed orange, red, pink, and purple as the sun sank into the Gulf of Mexico. Colonel Good and his cannon loomed as black shapes between Aaron and the dying sun. Aaron leaned well back into the shadows.

The colonel broke the silence. "What did you think you were doing, Matthews?"

"My job, sir. The one I've been given, not the one I would have chosen. Sir."

"Yes, yes, I know. The ignobility of it all. And what in God's name did you think you would do if you had not grounded on Pelican? Go on to Mobile?"

"Perhaps I would've been welcome there. I thought they picked me for this job because of my social connections in Charleston. I could have visited the homes of Confederate supporters—maybe even officers and politicians. I might even have done some good. ... Sir."

The colonel scoffed. "Until they caught you and hauled you before a Rebel firing squad. Your work is here. You will forego martyrdom for the time being, Lieutenant."

Aaron came to his feet, but before he could turn away the colonel wheeled to face Aaron and laid his spyglass gently but firmly on Aaron's shoulder.

"Tell me what you saw in the harbor when you left Havana," the colonel said.

"A couple of English-built sloops, very fast I think, and one frigate with nasty looking cannon."

"And you are not concerned, Lieutenant?"

"Ending this war is my concern, Colonel, and wasting my time and talents on this godforsaken, out-of-the-way piece of rock is not my idea of the way to do it." Aaron acknowledged the increased pressure of the spyglass on his shoulder and slumped back into his seat in the shadows.

Colonel Good slapped his telescope shut. "You want to end this war? Food, gunpowder, clothing, shoes, tools, weapons—I've got a shipment of LeMat grapeshot revolvers sent from France for issue to Confederate solders—these are the things that will end this war. The South has to ship raw materials out and finished goods back in, just like breathing. We can strangle it."

"Be my guest," said Aaron. "You don't need me or whoever's in Havana harbor."

"Wrong. I need you *because* of whoever's in Havana harbor. Practically everyone one on this island has closer ties to Havana harbor than you have to your own mother."

Aaron's tone was ironic. "That goes without saying."

"I'm sorry. I didn't mean..."

"Permission to withdraw, sir. I need to see to housing myself with the locals."

Colonel Good nodded and seemed tired as he turned away. "Is your brother well, Lieutenant?"

"With General Floyd's troops near Sewell Mountain last I heard, sir. Just another loyal son of the Confederate state of South Carolina."

"At least it must be some consolation that while you're here you will not be shooting at him," said the colonel.

"Let's stop this war before someone else shoots at him, sir. How shall I contact you?"

The colonel sighed. "See the ship's chandler, Curry. But be discreet. Goodnight, uh, what name are you using, again?"

"Matthews, sir."

"Well, goodnight, Matthews."

Aaron was halfway down the stone steps when the colonel called to him. "Aaron. Several of the officers and enlisted men have honorable intentions with regard to local ladies. I'll not tolerate complaints of defrauded debutantes. I shall expect you to exercise restraint."

"I'll try, sir." Aaron disappeared down the steps

and across the darkness of the parade ground.

...

At dawn the next morning, Josephine Marie Thibodeaux entered her brother Richard's bedroom expecting to find it unoccupied. She beamed with surprise and delight when she beheld a slumbering form behind the mosquito netting. Thinking Richard had somehow regained his sanity and stayed away from yesterday's war-bound English schooner, she leapt upon the sleeping form, hugging it about its middle.

"Wretched!" she cried happily.

The bed's occupant was shocked out of a sound sleep and bounded up to grapple with its attacker, sending them both to the floor in a tangle of bedclothes and mosquito netting.

After a frantic scramble, two heads burst from beneath the linens, one shouting "What are *you* doing here?" at the same time the other shouted "What the devil do you think—?"

Joe continued, "You're not Wretched!"

"As many ladies with ... intimate knowledge of me will attest," said Aaron Matthews with a grin.

They began untangling themselves from the bedclothes, Joe with the object of getting out of them—Aaron with the object of keeping at least a portion of them wrapped about his loins. The girl was fully clothed, but Aaron had been sleeping in the nude. Even in winter the nights were tropically warm on Key West.

"This is Richard's room!" declared Joe.

"Dear me, I understood it to be vacant. At least, that is what Captain Thibodeaux indicated when he let it to me last evening." Aaron finally succeeded in disengaging himself from her. He sat (appropriately swathed) on the bed while Joe backed across the room to press her posterior against the door.

"I had the impression from your parents," said Aaron, "that while your father and all the other wreckers were racing to the reef to save my unfortunate *St. Gertrude,* good old Wretched Richard was sneaking off to join the Glorious Army Of The Confederacy."

Joe was pressing door splinters into her backside in her haste to get out of the room. "I'm going turtling before it gets too light. I only came to get the poking stick ... here it is ... I'm sorry I disturbed you, Mister ..."

"Matthews. Joe, isn't it?"

"I gotta go. It'll be light." With that she slipped out the door and closed it behind her.

Aaron snatched up his clothes, from the chair where he had piled them, and jigged into them.

...

Minutes later, on a deserted beach, Joe had pulled the hem of her lightweight cotton dress between her legs, back-to-front, and tucked it into her belt to form blousy pantaloons. Her floppy straw hat brim flapped like wings in the breeze as she strolled along hard-packed sand at the water's edge, three-foot poking stick in one hand, boots dangling by their laces in the other.

"Good morning, again," said a familiar bass voice.

Startled, she looked up to see Matthews sitting in the soft sand at the base of a tree, plainly waiting for her.

She walked faster. "Mornin'."

Aaron stood, brushed the sand from his clothes, grabbed his shoes, and hurried to overtake her. He had gone to considerable effort to determine where she might have gone and to arrive ahead of her. He had not asked himself why; it simply seemed important at the time.

The morning sun burned brightly. Joe stopped, squinted against the glare, and gestured to the distant shoreline in dismay. "Oh, see! O-o-o-h, I knew it would be too late. It's all your fault. We could've turned her."

Aaron squinted in that direction. "Turned whom?"

Joe pointed. "The loggerhead. See, she's gone back to the sea. Just a minute sooner and we'd have caught her on the beach. Maybe she's laid!"

At that Joe dashed to the turtle's tread-like marks in the sand and began back-tracking them away from the water, poking at the soft sand on either side of the tracks with her stick.

Many yards from shore she emitted a squeal of delight and fell to her knees, digging furiously.

Aaron trudged through the soft sand to stand over her excavation.

"Take off your pants, Mister Matthews!" she

demanded, still digging.

"Young lady, not only am I shocked at that request, but I am unaccustomed to hearing it from people who do not know me well enough to call me by my Christian name."

Joe dug faster. "It's your fault we're late. The very least you can do is help."

"By taking off my pants?"

"You got drawers on, ain't ya?"

Aaron unbuckled his belt. "Indisputable logic if ever I heard it," he said.

Hanging his belt with its brass buckle over his shoulder, he stepped out of his pants and dropped them next to Joe on the sand. The heavy brass buckle of the belt dangling down his chest was wrought in the shape of initials: ABM.

Without giving him a second look, she tied knots in the legs of his pants, making them into a double-barreled sack, and began to fill the sack with turtle eggs.

Comprehending the goal, Aaron dropped to his knees and helped dig out the eggs and fill the makeshift sack.

"A hundred and ten!" Joe proclaimed. "Best me and Richard ever found was ninety. Cataline and Stepney fund a hundred and thirty-two one time."

"What will you do with them?"

The two stood up and, carrying the full pants between them, walked toward town.

"Sell 'em at the kraals," said Joe, using the local name for the commercial turtle pens on the north side of the island. The South African word, meaning a corral or pen for animals, had arrived in Key West via sailing ship, as all things did.

"Ah," said Aaron, wondering what "the crawls" might be. "And will they bring enough money that you might forgive the blackguard who cost you the turtle by making you late this morning?"

Joe smiled fully upon Aaron for the first time, and he was unprepared for its effect on him. Guilt showed in his face for an unguarded instant.

"Wretched would like you," Joe told him.

"High praise indeed," he said. He looked again at the eggs. "This reminds me, what do we do about breakfast?"

...

Fire was always a danger on Key West, with its wooden houses built so close together that gossip traveled from porch to porch with nobody being troubled to leave home in order to visit the neighbors. Cooking was done in small, separate structures built in back of the main house, so that kitchen fires did not spread to the home.

Later that morning, in the Thibodeaux kitchen building, Lucy Drake, a skinny black woman, was doing the baking before the day's heat reached its zenith.

The open doors at either end of the small white wood frame building revealed the rear yard of the Thibodeaux house, shaded with avocado, orange, mango, papaya, and banana trees interspersed with witch hazel, bougainvillea, and elephant ear plants.

Two goats grazed at the rear fence. Most Key West households kept a goat or two as convenient garbage disposals.

Joe's head appeared in an open doorway. "Mornin', Lucy! I'm starved."

Lucy went on about her work. "And well you might be, off fishing or crabbing while the whole world breakfasted! You might stay 'round and be some comfort to your mum just now ... her grievin' over poor Mister Richard gone off to war ... Good Lord, child! You stink like old mullet nets!"

Joe swung on the open door as she listened to Lucy's lecture then entered the kitchen, pulling Aaron behind her. "That stink ain't me, it's Mister Matthews's trousers. We found a loggerhead's nest on the beach this mornin'."

"I had drawers on...,"Aaron responded sheepishly to an accusing look from Lucy.

Lucy turned her look upon Joe with, "So, you've been to the kraals instead of eating breakfast like civilized young ladies."

"But look, Lucy!" Joe produced some coins from her pocket and pressed them into Lucy's flour-coated hand. "We can add it to the Freedom Fund." Joe turned to Aaron to say, "Cataline's going to marry Lucy soon as we can buy her papers from Mister Dennis."

Lucy gave Aaron a sideways glance and pocketed the coins.

"Aren't you going to put them—?" Joe protested.

Lucy cut her off, "I know what to do with them, Nosey Josey. You get on about your business and let working people get on about theirs."

"Speaking of business," said Aaron, "I believe I'd better get myself cleaned up and pay a visit to the honorable Judge Marvin at the admiralty court. See what may be left of my investment in the *St. Gertrude*. Miss Lucy, I fear these trousers have seen better days. Do you think you might be able to—?"

"Leave them out. Mister Richard used to come home in the same state. Nobody in town gets turtle stench out like Lucy Drake. Nor as often, seems to me!"

"Thank you," he said. "I'll pay you, of course."

Lucy was abrupt, apparently eager to be rid of him. "My wages is paid to Mister Dennis, sir," she said.

"Then perhaps you will allow me to make a small contribution to the, ah, Freedom Fund?"

Lucy ignored this. "You'll find fresh fried roe on the dining room sideboard under the linen towel. Scones and guava jelly on the table, and fruit in the basket."

Joe turned toward the house with considerable enthusiasm. "Thanks, Lucy. Come along, Mister Matthews."

Aaron doffed a nonexistent hat to Lucy as he left, but she looked up from her work only after he had gone. Her hand floated unconsciously to the pocket where Joe's coins rested.

After she was sure no one was within sight or

sound, Lucy loosened and removed a brick from the rustic hearth and hid her coins in the hole that constituted her Freedom Fund "safe."

...

Having breakfasted and dressed for business, Aaron Matthews walked the wide, sunny avenues of Key West until he stopped on Eaton Street across from a two-story white house built over an arch-covered brick carriageway. He looked left and right, decided this was the place, and crossed the street.

In the courtyard of the Arch House, Aaron entered via the brick carriageway, under the latticework arch, and followed a winding path through jungle-like foliage to a low, wooden building shaded with slatted Bahama shudders. It was a cigar factory. The air around it was redolent of rich tobacco, pineapple plants, and hibiscus blossoms. Aaron climbed the low steps and went inside.

Entering, he found himself in a cramped front room where Arnau, the swarthy, gnarled factory owner, hunched over a desk. A vividly multi-colored macaw perched behind the desk. Most of the long, narrow building was through a door opposite the one Aaron had used. He could see through that door a narrow room where sixteen men rolled cigars by hand at long tobacco-stained tables.

"You are Arnau?" asked Aaron.

The factory owner squinted up at him. "*En qué puedo servirle?*" he asked.

"My humidor is empty," Aaron replied. "Your sister in Havana told me you would fill it with the very best."

Arnau lost interest in the paperwork on his desk. His gaze was more direct now. "Do you keep an apple in your humidor, *señor*?"

Aaron answered, "Without one, even the best cheroot can become dry and tasteless."

Joe's voice came out of nowhere, "I didn't know you had a sister, Arnau!"

Both men's eyes swung to the interior doorway, where Joe was emerging from the factory proper. Arnau recovered first. "You think because you ask the million questions that Arnau tell you everything, *chiquita*? Even from you I have my secrets."

She smiled, accustomed to his teasing, and moved across the office toward the exterior door, exchanging a nod of greeting with Aaron. She called to the old man, "I'll see you tomorrow, if I can," and to the macaw, "Goodbye, Ulises."

The bird squawked, "*Buenos Días! Buenos Días!*"

Arnau mocked Joe's voice, "Goodbye, Arnau."

The door closed behind Joe as she exited. The room was quiet again. Aaron and Arnau exchanged a serious look. Arnau rose from his desk.

"Come," said the old man. "I show you the birds."

...

An hour later, in the white-bright sunshine on Tift's Wharf, Aaron, Captain Thibodeaux, William Curry, and a small group of townspeople, including two or three Yankee soldiers, watched the U.S. Marshal nail a notice to a warehouse wall. The placard read:

U.S. MARSHAL'S SALE

By virtue of an order of sale from the Hon. William Marvin, Judge of the Admiralty Court for the Southern District of Florida, I will sell at Public Auction on the 15th inst., from the Ware House of F.A. Browne, Esq., all the cargo then unredeemed by the payment of Salvage and expenses of the ship ST. GERTRUDE, lately wrecked on her voyage from Liverpool to New Orleans, Consisting of Iron in bars, crates of Crockery, Hard Ware, Sugar boilers, castings of Machinery, etc. Terms of sale—Cash on delivery—ten days to be allowed the purchaser to pay for and receive his goods. Consignees in Havana may have their goods delivered to them at any time before the day of sale, by the payment of Salvage and expenses.

J.B. BROWNE, U.S. MARSHAL
Key West, 4 April 1862.

The marshal completed his work, gathered up his tools, and turned to give the crowd an authoritative stare. They parted to allow him egress. Mr. Curry, a diminutive, mild-mannered Scots storekeeper, hopped birdlike alongside the departing marshal.

"You should specify 'No Confederate Currency.'

It's only good business, regardless of your personal politics," said Curry.

Marshal Browne, a notorious Confederate sympathizer, glared at the Scotsman and at the Yankee soldiers in the crowd then moved on without responding.

The crowd finished reading the notice and began to drift away. Thibodeaux, Curry, and Aaron were left.

Thibodeaux clapped Aaron across the shoulders, saying, "There you are, lad. In a few days it will all be liquidated and you'll have a fair amount left over after the fees are paid to the wrecking master—in this case, yours truly."

"A position Joe earned for you by getting you there first, you old lobster," teased Aaron. "Which, by the way, could be a bit suspicious, you know. How did you find us so quickly? Couldn't be you knew where the wreck would be because you knew where you'd laid the false light, could it?"

Thibodeaux rubbed his nose and grinned. "Any Conch worth his wrecking license can smell a salvageable vessel in the dark from miles away."

Curry tugged on Aaron's sleeve, and Aaron looked down into wire-rimmed spectacles.

"You are Mister Matthews, lately master of the ship *St. Gertrude?"* asked Curry.

"I am. May I assist you?"

Curry looked pointedly at Thibodeaux, who knew an unspoken request for privacy when he saw one.

"Well," said Thibodeaux, "I can't stand here jawing all day. If you gentlemen will excuse me." They nodded to one another, and Thibodeaux left.

When they were alone, the Scotsman said to Aaron, "I am William Curry. I operate the mercantile store and ships' chandlery. I'm to tell you to be at Colonel Good's office tonight after bellring. Now I must bid you good day."

Curry darted back to his store, leaving Aaron to murmur at empty air, "Good day, Mister Curry."

...

That night after the 8:00 p.m. curfew bell rang sending the Conchs to their homes, Aaron Matthews slipped past a young, sleepy sentry into Fort Taylor's parade grounds. Moments later Colonel Good reacted to a knock on the door of his quarters, rose from his desk, and admitted Aaron. "Were you seen?" the colonel asked.

Aaron wagged his head a quick no. "Everyone seems to watch the sea more than the land. What's the news?"

"I had hoped you would tell me. I confess I was piqued that you didn't tell me first."

Aaron looked confused. "Tell you what?"

Colonel Good opened a desk drawer and produced the leg band from a carrier pigeon. Unfolding the message contained therein, he handed it to Aaron, who moved closer to the lantern to read it.

"One of my men was hunting at dusk," said the colonel, "and got this one by mistake. I have cautioned him to avoid anything that looks even vaguely like a messenger pigeon in the future. Now kindly decode that for me and let me in on your discoveries to date."

Aaron continued to stare at the message paper, front and back, in light and in shadow. He answered without looking at the colonel. "It will take a while to decode it, but I can tell you now what I've discovered—and you may have given your marksman bad advice."

CHAPTER 4

"What the hell are you talking about?" Colonel Good asked.

"Someone else is sending messages to Havana," said Aaron. "This was not my bird. We've got ourselves a Confederate spy on our charming little island."

Colonel Good looked stricken. He and Aaron exchanged a look acknowledging the unspoken truth: We've got trouble.

Colonel Good paced the length of the room, deep in thought, while Aaron studied the coded message. At last, the colonel stopped in front of Aaron. "What do you think it says?"

Aaron sighed. "I'd guess he's telling the Rebel Navy what I'd tell them if I were in his boots. How much contraband you have. How many men to protect it—and how many of them are sick with yellow fever—"

Colonel Good drew a breath as if he would deny

this, but Aaron went on before the colonel could speak, "—Oh, yes, the state of your infirmary is passed from porch to porch with all the other Key West gossip."

Colonel Good began pacing again.

Aaron studied the message, thinking what else it might contain. "Or maybe I'd tell them how little fresh water you have. Or how much powder and shot."

"He couldn't know all that!" said the colonel.

"He'd find out," said Aaron. "I would."

The colonel digested this. "Well, however much he knows, he could not say much in that single message."

Aaron folded the message and stuffed it behind his initialed belt buckle. "Exactly," he said. "He may have sent other messages before now. And he'll most certainly send more in the future."

Colonel Good stopped before a wall map of the lower keys, Florida Straits, Forts Jefferson and Taylor, and Cuba. He traced a course from Havana harbor to Key West with his finger. The two islands appeared close to one another. Dangerously close. He gritted his teeth and growled, "Find him, Aaron!"

"I shall make good use of our advantage, sir," Aaron said as he nodded and started for the door.

The colonel stopped him, outrage boiling over, snapping, "Advantage! I see no advantage! Too much to protect and too few to protect it. Low water supplies and the wet season still months away. Yellow fever stealing men from my ranks. And now—," he jabbed the map's Havana harbor with stiff fingers, "Now a Rebel wolf pack growling at my door and a traitor among us waiting for the chance to let them in! What advantage?"

Aaron put his hand to the doorknob and smiled. "I know about *him*. But he doesn't know about me."

Aaron slipped out the door and left the fort as he had come, unheard and unseen.

Colonel Good turned again to look at the map. His fingers traced the outline of Havana harbor. "And who was waiting for your news, little bird?" the colonel muttered. "What will he do when you don't arrive? I wonder."

...

At dawn on the island of Cuba a young Rebel soldier climbed a twisting pig trail to the top of the bluffs overlooking the Florida Straits. He stopped to look out at the Caribbean-green waters, shielded his eyes from the blinding sunrise, and scanned the horizon for something that simply wasn't there.

After a few minutes of watching for something that would not appear, the soldier gave up. Dropping his hand wearily, he turned to trudge across the top of the bluff. His destination was a thatch-roofed shack seemingly built of driftwood, leaning next to an extensive pigeon coop. The residents of the coop cooed, fluttered, and scratched about in its depths, responding to the attentions of a small, dark, eccentric-looking Cuban peasant called Javi.

Hearing the soldier's boots scrape gravel, Javi

looked up. "What you want here so early?"

"Thought maybe it came," said the soldier with a shrug.

"These are pigeons, *amigo,* not owls. They don't fly all night, not even for you," Javi said with a chuckle.

Tired and obviously disappointed, the soldier turned and retraced his steps back down the jagged trail toward to foot of the bluffs.

...

It was also dawn on the other side of the Florida Straits, on the dirt streets of Key West. Morning mist hung among the mangrove roots and low-drooping banyan trees. The man on lookout lolled in the Tift's Wharf bell tower after a long night of watching for ships in distress.

A squarely built Cuban milkman led a cow from house to house, its neck-bell clanking as they sauntered. A 9-year-old slave girl came to the curb with an empty pitcher. The milkman stopped, to milk the cow directly into her container, and collected his coin.

A lanky black fisherman hawked freshly caught mullet from a basket balanced on his head. Lucy Drake waved to him from the Thibodeaux house, and he came to kneel and clean part of his catch for her on her kitchen steps.

Here a window was shoved open, there a curtain was drawn. Somewhere a goat bleated, a door slammed. The city was waking.

In Aaron's bedroom, yellow sunlight crept

across the room from the wooden-louvered windows, slunk over the head and shoulders of Aaron Matthews sleeping humped over Richard Thibodeaux's desk. A spent candle, dribbled wax mounded at its base, told of a long night—as did the pages of notes scribbled and crumpled under Aaron's elbows on the desktop.

A knock at the door jerked Aaron awake. Realizing where he was, he made a frantic sweep of the desk to hide his work from the visitor. "Come in."

Joe Thibodeaux made a careful entrance, taking in Aaron's rumpled clothing, still-made bed, and unshaven face. "You haven't slept?" she said.

Aaron gestured to the chair. "No, I ... I slept..."

"You all right?" said Joe. "Something wrong?"

"No. Not at all. Just paperwork. No end of paperwork."

Joe nodded. Maybe it meant she understood, maybe it didn't. "Mm-hmm," she said. "Auction coming up and all."

"Yes," Aaron pounced on that excellent explanation. "Exactly."

Joe backed out of the room without taking her eyes off him. "Breakfast'll be ready time you get shaved," she said.

He nodded his thanks, and she left. Aaron turned to the rumpled papers and took up one—the culmination of his night's labors. He folded it carefully and stuffed it behind his belt buckle, crushing the remaining pages into his pockets.

Minutes later Aaron emerged onto the back porch, clean-shaven, dressed, and ready to face the day. He looked around, saw no one, and headed toward the kitchen structure in the back yard.

Entering the kitchen, and seeing no one about, he went to the brick hearth (the only fireplace on the property) and quickly emptied his pockets of the decoding papers he had worked on all night. He watched the fire gobble them up then was startled to hear: "I've 'ad your trousers soaking." Lucy spoke from the doorway. "You can 'ave 'em back tomorrow."

Aaron covered his surprise like the professional he was. "That's quite all right," he said, smiling. "I merely came to thank you for another marvelous meal."

"You're welcome," she said. She didn't believe a man freshly dressed for business would go out of his way to stand in a sooty kitchen waiting to tell a slave woman thanks for the breakfast. She said nothing more.

Sensing no rapport developing, Aaron glanced back at the fire to be certain no traces of his work remained, then he moved past the stoic Lucy toward the kitchen door. "Yes, well. Always a pleasure, Miss Lucy," he said. "Good day."

In silence, Lucy watched him go.

...

Meanwhile, 90 miles to the south, in the captain's cabin of a Rebel ship, the commanding officer and his executive officer huddled over a desk strewn with maps and charts. They shuffled papers, compared one chart with another, measured distances, made notes on still more papers, and appeared to be concocting a plan.

Into this tense atmosphere came the Rebel soldier who had fruitlessly climbed the bluffs at dawn.

The commanding officer looked at him. "Well?"

The soldier shook his head. Nothing.

The C.O. deflated.

"Are we certain of the schedule?" asked the Exec. "Maybe it's not due until today ... or tomorrow."

"The bird was due yesterday," said the C.O. "Something must have happened to it."

"Or to our agent," inserted the soldier.

The C.O. reflected on this but rejected the idea. "Not likely," he said. "We'll just have to go with the information we have up to now, and hope that the next message gets through."

CHAPTER 5

As Aaron approached the door of Will Curry's mercantile store, he met Lila Dauthier coming out of that establishment—on the arm of a Union officer. Aaron doffed his hat in greeting.

"Good morning, Miss Dauthier," Aaron said.

"Good morning, Mister Matthews!" Lila put her officer forward like a trophy. "May I present my friend, Lieutenant R.B. Locke, from New York. The lieutenant is the editor and publisher of Key West's newspaper, the *New Era*."

Aaron extended a hand, which Locke took while somehow seeming to keep his distance.

"It's a pleasure to meet a member of the fourth estate, Lieutenant Locke," said Aaron pleasantly. "I didn't realize the Army was in the journalism business now."

Locke stood straighter. "We are since the Secesh propagandists had the good sense to leave Key

West," he said.

Lila gushed, "Lieutenant Locke is so knowledgeable about simply *everything.* I think it's so *stimulating* the way a journalist seems to fairly *vibrate* in tune with the *pulse* of a community."

"No doubt," said Aaron with a smile. If Lila was trying to make him jealous, her cause was hopeless. Aaron had never cared enough about a woman to be concerned when other men pursued her. Silently he wished them happy.

Locke began directing his flirtatious partner onward to other business, with a curt nod of farewell to Aaron. Lila waved prettily, and Aaron honored her with a courtly bow.

Once inside Curry's store, Aaron made his way between tables and shelves stacked with merchandise, much of it the cargo of ships wrecked in recent months on the reefs near Key West. Will Curry acknowledged Aaron with a nod but cautioned him with a sideways look at the customers in the store. Aaron saw Caroline Lowe and Mrs. Lowe as well as Josephine Marie Thibodeaux with friend (and parcel-bearer), Joseph Porter. The women were pawing through bolts of fabric—all of it the same color.

"Honestly," mewled Caroline, "I don't know why we have to keep looking. It's all the same."

Porter cautioned Joe, "That one has a water spot."

"Where?" she said, looking where he pointed. "Oh, yes. Thanks."

Caroline went on, "Wouldn't it be lovely to live in a town where nobody else had a dress exactly like yours?"

"Hush, child," said her mother. "Young ladies in Tallahassee are making their own hats out of palmetto fronds and crocheting their own shoes from scraps of baling twine. We'll take this one." She heaved a bolt of cloth from the bottom of the pile and plunked it on Curry's counter. She and Curry consummated the transaction, oblivious to the young people's further conversation.

"Tallahassee?" said Caroline. "We don't know anybody in Tallahassee. I've never even *been* to Florida."

"This is Florida, Caroline," said Joe then consulted with Porter further: "I can't decide. Maybe the one with the water spot is more ... interesting."

Porter looked tired.

Aaron stepped from behind piles of merchandise with a greeting, "Miss Thibodeaux."

The three shoppers reacted in different ways. Joe showed surprise and pleasure, Caroline curiosity and anticipation, and Porter suspicion with a touch of jealousy.

"Why Mister Matthews," said Joe, beaming. "You should have told me you needed something. I could have saved you a walk."

"Nonsense," he said. "It was worth the walk to meet such lovely ladies." He turned to Caroline, "Aaron Matthews, at your service, ma'am."

Porter looked relieved that Aaron's attentions had been directed elsewhere. It was Joe's turn to feel the green-eyed monster tickle her innards.

Caroline's eyes lit up when Aaron greeted her. "You came in the *St. Gertrude*!" she said.

"Guilty."

"I am so pleased to make your acquaintance, Mister Matthews. Tell me, were there any textiles among your goods?" Caroline had never knowingly missed an opportunity to expand her wardrobe.

A short time later, Caroline Lowe and Mrs. Lowe, with their parcels, exited Curry's store onto the street just as the familiar Sergeant Pfifer and his blue-clad patrol were striding past. Caroline couldn't resist teasing them.

"Good day, Sergeant," she chirped.

"Miss Lowe. Miz Lowe," Pfifer replied without missing a step.

The patrol went its way, the ladies theirs, but the last soldier to pass could not resist looking toward the roof of the Lowe house, just in case.

Back inside Curry's store, Joe and Porter had finished their shopping and prepared to leave. Aaron stepped into their path with an eye to their parcels.

"Need any help with that?" Matthews offered.

"I can handle it, thank you," was Porter's quick retort.

"Porter can handle it," said Joe, more pleasantly. "But thank you just the same."

Aaron nodded. "Well, then," he said. "Perhaps

I'll see you later, Miss Thibodeaux. If you're not out turtling." He winked. He refused to question his motives. She was an attractive female, if slightly younger than the experienced courtesans he generally preferred. But she was no child and, therefore, was fair game.

Joe smiled, secretly reveling in the sharing of a private joke with this man.

Porter pressed forward saying, "Good day, Mister Matthews," and wasted no time getting Joe out of the store and away from the competition.

When they had gone, Aaron leaned on Curry's counter, fished the decoded message out from behind his belt buckle, and folded it into Curry's hand.

"Will you be sending a delivery to the fort today?" Aaron asked.

"Aye, if it's something they need," the Scotsman answered.

"It is. Now, if I wanted to know something about homing pigeons, who would I ask?"

Curry thought then said, "You could ask Arnau, the cigar maker..."

Aaron wagged his head. Arnau was his own bird keeper. He sought the keeper of his enemy's pigeons.

Curry thought harder and came up with an alternative. "Sandy Cornish. A free man of color. Down off the end of Whitehead Street, in the colored quarter. Look for the best vegetable garden in town. That's Sandy's place."

Aaron made a mental note, shook Curry's hand, and headed for the door. He had another idea and stopped. "And if I wanted to know about setting a false light on just the right beach at just the right time, who would I ask?"

To his credit, Curry resisted the urge to quip, "Anybody on the island." Instead he said, "Captain John Geiger. Retired. Does nothing but tend his flowers and watch the reefs. He has seen a trick or two in his time, I'll wager. I'll not say he done 'em, but he surely seen 'em. And he has no love for the Confederates nor the Yanks. Key West Conch through and through he is. Big white house straight up Whitehead Street, that way."

...

Behind the white picket fence at Geiger's house the rainbow colors of a carefully kept flower garden ran riot. A lush green moat of plant life surrounded wide verandas front and rear of the three-story white house. Aaron stepped up to the front gate.

"Ahoy! State your business!" boomed a voice.

Aaron looked to all points of the compass and finally upward. There in the rooftop widow's walk was a doughy septuagenarian whose white hair billowed in the sea breeze. Aaron knew this must be John Geiger.

"Ahoy, yourself!" Aaron called, smiling. "My name is Matthews, I— "

"You came in the *St. Gertrude!"* Geiger announced.

"That's right. Can we talk about it?"

"The *St. Gertrude*?" teased Geiger, "Or the bonfire that made an ass of her captain?"

Aaron's smile turned ironic. "The *St. Gertrude* is a lost cause, I'm afraid, but perhaps we can still save the ass of her captain."

Geiger liked this. He laughed, and waves of glee rippled head to toe through his hefty frame. He motioned to Aaron to come up onto the roof. Aaron mounted the front steps, entered the house, and climbed the interior staircase.

...

Aaron Matthews and John Geiger talked as easily as old friends, and in the silences they each lounged against the railings of the widow's walk and enjoyed the sight, sound, and smell of the sea.

They had been together for some time, and Aaron was idly studying the streets of town with Geiger's spyglass.

Geiger was saying, "So, whoever he was, he loves money enough to perform the unethical, the unforgiveable, and the illegal to get it. Any man who loves it that much won't be able to wait long to spend it. You watch for a man with low morals and high expenditures. He's your fire-starter."

Something on the street arrested Aaron's attention and caused him to focus more carefully with the spyglass. After getting a thorough look for himself, Aaron handed the glass to Captain Geiger and moved to exit the widow's walk.

"Excuse me," Aaron said, "I believe I have an

appointment." He was halfway down the interior stairs when he called back, "Thank you, Captain. You've been a great help."

John Geiger registered mild surprise at Aaron's abrupt departure. He turned the spyglass in the direction Aaron had been looking, and he saw what had caused the sudden activity. Geiger smiled broadly and murmured, "If you'll take my advice, you won't let her mother catch you!"

...

Minutes later, on the beach, Josephine Marie sat propped against a tree near the spot where Aaron had intercepted her once before. She wore her turtling clothes, and her poking stick leaned on the tree behind her.

While Joe watched the surf, a hand snaked from behind the foliage and stole her poking stick. The poking stick—sharply pointed and dangerous-looking—moved ominously toward a spot between her shoulder blades. At the last instant, instead of stabbing her in the back, the stick flicked upward, catching the brim of Joe's sunhat and tumbling it into her lap.

Accustomed to holding her own against an older brother, Joe whipped around, knife in hand, to find Aaron's grin waiting for her. She settled back onto the sand, slipping her knife back into her boot. Aaron emerged from the plants and sat beside her.

"I had decided you weren't coming," she said.

"I didn't really believe you would come until I

saw you leave the house. Nearly broke my neck getting here," said Aaron.

After a short, thoughtful silence, Joe said, "Why, do you think?"

"Because you had a good head start on me, that's why," Aaron quipped. *Why indeed?* He refused to try to answer that question.

"No," she said, "I mean, why do you think either of us came at all? Two unmarried people, alone, in the middle of the day when anybody might see us. This is the worst idea ever, and yet I was caught in it like a fly in honey the minute you said something about turtling this afternoon. My reputation would be ruined forever, and you would at least lose your lodgings—if not some blood."

"It isn't my intention to compromise you." He surprised himself, realizing it was true. He had never been concerned about such a thing before today. Of course, the women with whom he dealt were older, worldly, sophisticated.

"I know that."

She absolutely trusted him, and he found that absolutely frightening. "Do you want me to leave?" He didn't know how he would force himself to do so, but he had to make the offer.

"No," she said. "I want you to tell me everything's fine, and nobody knows or cares what we do."

She looked to him for an answer. He looked back with a weak smile and a tiny side-to-side movement of his head. He didn't have an answer that would satisfy. Or, if he did, he had no idea how to say it.

Their gaze held for a moment, then both resorted to studying the reefs beyond the shore. Aaron made designs in the sand with Joe's stick.

They shared some quiet minutes, then Joe said, "Your ship is English registry."

"Was, yes." Mundane conversation. This was a relief. This he knew how to do.

"So, you're from Liverpool?" she guessed.

"Now, how would you know—? Ah, of course, the wrecker's daughter. You probably know more than I do about the shipping business." He sounded proud of her knowledge, and they exchanged a quick smile. "Yes, I sailed from Liverpool," he said. "By way of Havana, of course."

Again they watched the sea. Gulls shrieked overhead. The poking stick swished to and fro in the sugary sand. Dry palm branches scraped as the wind used them to polish the trunks of the trees.

"When do you think your country will officially recognize the Confederacy as a nation?" asked Joe.

Aaron sighed. She meant England, he knew, but England was not his country. "My country," he began, "my country is ... divided on that question for the moment."

War. Business. Friendships. Family. Secrets. Trust. Each other. Thoughts of all these matters whirled through their heads as they sat together, growing more and more aware of the impossibility of it all.

Joe shook off her reverie and came to her feet. She held out a hand to Aaron, who looked up with a question in his eyes.

"I need to walk," she explained.

He took her hand and rose to walk with her down the empty beach. Reluctantly, once he was standing he relinquished the warmth of her small hand in his. They strolled side-by-side, carefully not touching one another.

The White House – Washington, D.C.

President Lincoln worked at annotating one document after another from the tidy stacks spread across his desk. At the same time, he seemed to be half-listening to one of his trusted advisers. The middle-aged, mustachioed adviser was leaning across the desk as if to force his logic onto the president by weight of proximity. Anxiety caused an involuntary vibrato in the adviser's voice.

"Mister President," the adviser said, "the sooner the proclamation is issued, the better. Every morning I fear I'll wake up to news that the English have granted official diplomatic status to the Confederate States."

"Thank God that you, at least, wake up," said Lincoln. "Thousands of fine young men no longer enjoy that luxury." He continued to work on his papers.

The adviser, unable to stand still, moved about the room as he continued to state his case.

"I know that, sir, and I'm not belittling their sacrifice. I'm merely saying if England recognizes the Confederacy, can France be far behind? And other countries as well? What will it do to our chances of reuniting our nation when the rest of the world formally decrees that two nations, not one, exist on our soil? Issue the proclamation. Make this a war against slavery. Then the Confederacy's position will be too heinous, too unpopular for the Europeans ever to recognize them."

Lincoln fixed him with a withering stare. "Do you think I don't know that?" he said. "Do you think I postpone freeing the southern slaves on a whim? Yes, the proclamation must be issued. The United States must denounce the Confederates' allegiance to slavery as a way of life. But our indignation must appear to be genuine. To announce such a thing while we continue to lose battle after battle would sound like exactly what it would be—a desperate cry for help."

The adviser returned to the edge of the desk to look the president squarely in the eye. "We can't afford many more battles like Shiloh, sir. We claimed victory on the field, but we lost thirteen thousand men to the Rebels' ten thousand."

"How well I know it."

"Sir, if we don't make this war too dirty for the English, it may be hopeless."

"Agreed," said the president. "Show me a significant Union victory, or even a stalemate that I can call a victory. Then I'll sign the Emancipation."

The Beach – Key West, Florida

Joe and Aaron had walked a long time on the beach. Their footprints stretched behind them into the distance. They seemed content just to be in the same place, together.

"I'm looking for the man who set that light on Boca Chica," Aaron said softly, knowing the culprit might be Joe's friend or relative, or even she herself.

"I know," she said.

"I know you said you had nothing to do with that," he said, "but you can understand how it looks. I mean, clearly you would have done anything to help your brother escape."

Joe stopped him and searched his face. "What would you have done if your brother wanted more than anything to fight for his country?"

Thinking of his own brother, Aaron spoke the absolute truth for once. "I would have done everything in my power to keep him home, safe. Everything."

Joe shook off his words and began walking again. Aaron came even with her and put his arm around her shoulder.

Tears glinted in her eyes as she said, "Richard could've stayed home and done his duty right here if the Secesh had thrown the mudsills out of Fort Taylor when they had the chance."

There was no reply. They simply continued making ambling footprints down the beach.

...

That night inside the fort, Colonel Good was cleaning his sidearm when a quick knock at the door was followed immediately by Aaron Matthews' slipping inside.

"News?" asked the colonel.

Aaron shook his head, moved to the desk, took his own Army Colt from the waistband at his back, and sat down to clean it using the colonel's materials.

The colonel frowned at Aaron's Colt. "Now, how do you expect to explain that, when you're supposed to be a civilian in a town under martial law?"

Aaron put a finger to his lips. "Sh-h-h-h-h." He indicated he didn't expect the gun to be discovered. After a moment he said, "I'll be sending a bird off tomorrow, to let my contact in Jamaica know something's up in Havana, and to tell them they won't be hearing from me for a few days."

"And then?"

"Can you post a marksman to watch the southern coastline for pigeons for the next several days?"

The colonel smiled. "If our friend mails a letter, we'll see it doesn't get delivered."

CHAPTER 6

Tropical sun and blue sky hovered over mid-morning on Key West. The milkman's cow no longer added her bell's lazy clang to the cries of the peripatetic fishmonger going from house to house with his night's catch.

Aaron Matthews walked up to the gate of the Geiger house, but before he could enter, a movement caught his eye. Turning, he watched Joe Thibodeaux dash across a distant intersection, headed into the Cuban quarter of town. Curiosity wrinkled his brow. He followed her.

Joe stopped on the street outside the Arch House and looked quickly left and right. Aaron, a few yards behind her, ducked behind a banyan tree. From there he saw her dart through the latticed archway of the two-story white house and into the brick-pathed courtyard beyond.

Once in the courtyard, Joe traversed the brick

walkway to the low wooden building shaded by Bahama-shuttered windows. Cats and chickens came to see if she had food for them, and she cooed to them in greeting but kept moving—to the door of the cigar factory.

Joe entered the small room where Arnau hunched over his desk fussing with incomprehensible paperwork. The rainbow-colored macaw perched behind him squawked, *"Buenos Días! Buenos Días!"*

Joe went immediately to the bird, scarcely seeing Arnau. *"Buenos Días, Ulises!"* said Joe.

Arnau said without looking up, *"Y Buenos Días, Arnau?"*

"Y Buenos Días, Arnau. Has he learned any new words this week?"

"A few, perhaps. But you have no time for foolish birds now. Carmen is very tired. You are late again."

Joe was already heading for the larger room that comprised most of the shady building. "I'm sorry," she said. "My mother ... sometimes it's hard to get away."

Outside, Aaron slipped into the courtyard and moved quietly down the brick walkway, stopping to pet a kitten and take a slow look around.

Inside, Joe entered a large room where sixteen Cuban men sat at long wooden tables stacked with tobacco leaves. Each man was an artist, rolling and stacking cigars with brown-stained fingers, constantly in motion, never looking up. Hour upon hour they rolled, clipped, stacked, rolled, clipped, stacked; and the piles of tobacco leaves on the left gradually became the countless cigars on the right.

At the far end of the room, near a window, a thirty-something Cuban woman sat on a high stool and read to the workers. She was in the middle of a thick book. Other books were stacked beside the stool, as was a guitar. Sometimes the workers were treated to music in lieu of a story.

Joe walked past the long tables toward the stool as Carmen read: "'I am the girl that dragged little Oliver back to old Fagin's on the night he went out from the house in Pentonville.'"

When Joe reached the stool, Carmen looked up gratefully, changed places with Joe, and handed Joe the book.

Joe looked at it. "*Oliver Twist.* New?"

"From the captain of the English schooner. He loves Arnau's cheroots."

Carmen left as Joe began to read: " ' "You!" said Rose Maylie. "I, lady!" replied the girl. "Thank Heaven upon your knees that you had friends to care for and keep you in your childhood and that you were never in the midst of cold and hunger..." '."

Outside the cigar factory, Aaron Mathews explored the distant corners of the courtyard, including a wire mesh enclosure where Arnau kept a dovecote. Aaron had just reached the pigeon coop when he heard a door close at the front of the building. He ducked behind a plant and watched as Carmen exited the building and proceeded through the archway toward the street.

When she was gone, he hurriedly selected a pigeon from the coop, affixed a band from his pocket to its leg, and tossed it skyward.

Assured that his message was on its way, Aaron prowled along the back wall of the long low building, crouching from window to window, listening to Joe's voice.

"'I have stolen away from those who would surely murder me if they knew I had been here, to tell you what I have overheard. Do you know a man named...'"

Aaron registered alarm. He tripped over a kitten that was winding between his feet seeking company. The kitten yowled and, in the attempt to regain his balance without giving himself away, Aaron missed part of Joe's narrative. What he heard when he recovered alarmed him more—at first:

"'...he goes by some other than his own name among us, which I more than thought before. Some time ago, and soon after Oliver was put into your house on the night of the robbery...'."

Aaron's brow curled in confusion at this...

"'...I—suspecting this man—listened to a conversation between him and Fagin in the dark ...'."

Relief flooded Aaron's body, relaxing clenched muscles, as he recognized the story. The new Dickens novel, *Oliver Twist,* had been all the rage in England when Aaron was there. Joe was not preparing to announce the presence of a spy on the island, she was merely reading aloud to the cigar makers.

Joe continued to read *Oliver Twist.* Aaron settled into the plants beneath the window, listening to the story. The kitten came and cuddled in his lap, and he stroked it absently, absorbed in Joe's voice. He was unaccountably happy and refused to analyze his reasons.

...

The glare was bright and hot off the Florida Straits, and on the bluffs of the Cuban coast a young Rebel soldier hunkered on the ground outside the ramshackle hut of Javi, the pigeon man. The hut's crooked door creaked on its rusty hinges, and Javi emerged to squat beside the soldier. Javi carried a sloppy handful of roast fowl. He took a bite then offered some to the soldier, who declined.

"Wouldn't you think we'd have had some word by now?" asked the soldier.

"Why? You think big news? You think *los inglés* say to *los yanquis* to leave your country alone because you have *amigos* in London now? I don't think so, *mi general.*"

The young soldier was far too earnest to appreciate Javi's teasing. "No, not yet at least," he said. "We've got to show ourselves strong. We've got to reclaim our ports—most of all New Orleans."

Javi stopped eating to take a swig from a raggedy wineskin and wipe his mouth on his hairy forearm. "*Ay, Nueva Orleans!* I went there once. A man can find anything he wants in *Nueva Orleans.* I hope to go back there someday."

"So do we," the soldier said. "Go back there with a fleet of our ships and blow the Yankee Navy to kingdom come. But we've got to get past Key West first. And that's the news I'm waitin' on. Where the Sam Hill is that bird from Key West?" The soldier stood and, shading his eyes with one hand, made an even more serious search of the horizon northward. Nothing but sun, sky, and blue-green water.

Javi gestured with the remains of the roasted bird in his hand. "Either your friend in Key West didn't have no news to send you, or he have news to send you, but the bird he send is ver', ver' slow. Me, I don't keep the slow ones." He bit again into his (presumably slow) avian lunch.

CHAPTER 7

At the same hour, in Curry's store, William Curry wrapped a purchase in brown paper and twine while Aaron Matthews waited to take it home. Finishing, Curry handed the package to Matthews, who began to walk away. Curry stopped him.

"Your change, sir. Don't be forgettin' your change."

It was a baldfaced lie. Aaron turned a questioning look on Curry, who nodded to a pair of customers browsing a few feet away. Understanding the reason for the deception, Aaron then followed Curry to a counter at the rear of the store.

Curry reached into a drawer and dropped a half-dozen glittering gemstones into the palm of Aaron's hand. He spoke for Aaron's ears alone: "Colored drayman, works for W.D. Cash, my competitor up the street, gave me these in payment of a debt."

Aaron pocketed the stones before anyone else

could chance to look his way. "Why didn't he just give you money?" asked Aaron. "Why risk giving himself away like this, paying you with stones you would know were stolen?"

"I never accept Confederate currency, and that is all Noah Lewis ever has to offer. 'No, thank you very much,' I say, 'it's not good business, regardless of your personal politics.'"

Sounds of the front door opening and feminine giggling interrupted, as Lila Dauthier and her latest Yankee conquest, Colonel Morgan, entered the store. Lila saw Aaron and made a beeline toward him, Morgan in tow.

Aaron had to talk fast. "What did you say his name was?"

Lila was close enough to hear Curry's response. Aaron would not realize the significance of that proximity until much later.

"Noah Lewis," Curry said.

Aaron murmured to Curry, "I'll find him." Then he turned his attention to Lila. "Good day, Miss Dauthier."

"Mister Matthews. May I present Colonel Joseph Morgan?"

The two men exchanged a handshake and nod of acknowledgment as Lila chattered on. "Colonel Morgan will be commanding Fort Taylor in the coming weeks while Colonel Good is temporarily in South Carolina."

Aaron was moving toward the door with his parcel, leaving Lila and Morgan to their shopping.

"Really. Then I'm sure you and I will meet again, Colonel."

Morgan eyed Aaron coldly and responded, "I'm almost certain of it."

Aaron exited the shop.

Lila turned to William Curry.

"I require a substantial—but attractive—parasol, Mister Curry," Lila proclaimed. "Despite everyone's assurances to the contrary, I'm convinced this lovely dry weather cannot last forever."

...

That night inside Fort Taylor, Morgan's quarters were damp and noisy. Thunder rattled the wooden shutters at the windows. A knock vibrated the pine door like the thunder's echo. Without waiting for response, Aaron Matthews hastened through the door, draped in a black slicker and dripping puddles on the coquina-stone floor. Rain pounded the ground outside—louder through the open door, then fading when the door closed. Lila's "lovely dry weather" had disappeared as she predicted.

Morgan, reading in bed, did not trouble himself over Aaron's arrival, saying merely, "Don't douse the candle."

Aaron was wet and irritable. "This couldn't have waited until tomorrow night?" he growled.

"I will not listen to complaints about the rain," said Morgan. "Our cistern is up eight inches already, and I hope by tomorrow morning to have an adequate supply of fresh water for the first time in months."

Aaron shucked his slicker and started toward several different chairs, abandoning each one, before finally dropping the wet slicker on the floor in a corner. He came to stand at the foot of Morgan's bed—but Morgan motioned him to back up a pace. He was still wet. His patience had washed away.

"Well, what have you got?" Aaron demanded.

"My hands full, thank you, with Colonel Good gone to South Carolina, a third of my men sick with fever, and you engaged in some wild goose chase—or wild pigeon chase, or whatever it is."

"Did you stop one or not?" Aaron spat through clinched jaws.

"On the table. For what it's worth."

Aaron turned to the table in the center of the room, scooped up a pigeon legband from beside the sputtering candle, and, holding it in his fist, looked at Morgan.

"'That's *it*?"

"'The rain has solved one of my problems, Lieutenant. I look to you to solve another. That is all."

Aaron pocketed the legband, snatched up his wet slicker from the corner, and stalked bitterly from the room, admitting the storm's roar once again when he opened the door.

At the Thibodeaux house the storm raged against the blackness as Aaron hurried up the front walk toward the porch steps. Wind whined, neighboring houses groaned and creaked, thunder boomed, and lightning flashed—casting grotesque shadows through the twisted banyan trees. Overhead a palm frond cracked like a shot and fell to hang limp alongside the trunk of the tree. Coconuts crashed like cannonballs to the ground, and Aaron dodged a near miss by one of them.

Wet and shivering, he reached the front door—never locked—and went in.

Inside the front parlor, Aaron removed his wet slicker and, braving the wind long enough to open the door again, dumped the slicker outside on the porch. He ducked back into the dry parlor, felt his way to a table, and struck a match from his pocket to light the oil lamp.

"Don't!" someone said.

Aaron nearly knocked the lamp over and, while righting it, burned his fingers and dropped the match.

"Great Caesar's ghost, woman! You scared the life out of me! You'll have me burning the house down!"

"I'm sorry, just ... please, don't light the lamp."

Lightning flashed, illuminating the parlor through the lace curtains at the windows. In the fleeting light Aaron could see Joe curled up, tight and small, at one end of the settee. She wore a modest, high-necked, long-sleeved white cotton nightgown.

"What are you doing down here at this hour, young lady? You should have been in bed long ago."

"I was," said Joe, "but ... but mother's room is

just below mine, and she mustn't hear me. So I came ... came down here. I didn't know you were out. I never meant to ... never meant to startle you—"

Lightning strobed the room again, and thunder roared, rattling the house on its foundations. Joe shivered and buried her head with her arms. Aaron sat down beside her and lifted her arms aside, forcing her to look at him.

"You've been crying!" he said. "What happened to that intrepid sailor who brought the *Lady Alyce* to my aid on the reefs?"

Lightning flashed again, and thunder cracked louder than ever.

Joe panicked and lunged against Aaron's chest.

"Please! Please, don't tell anybody!" she begged.

Aaron pushed her shoulders away from him long enough to remove his wet shirt. Then Aaron put his arms around her and drew her against his bare chest. "I never kiss and tell," he said.

When next the lightning bathed the room in its eerie white, Aaron and Joe were entwined on the settee, sharing a kiss that grew deeper and deeper. All thought of the storm outside was soon replaced by a conflagration inside; a fire they built in one another.

CHAPTER 8

Dawn on nearby Boca Chica island was amazingly calm after the storm of the previous night.

Diamonds of rainwater sparkled on broad, shiny-wet leaves of jungle plants. Birds bathed, chirping and splashing, in the red center-cups of huge pineapple-like bromeliads. Runoff from last night's storm plop-plopped from the tall trees and made water circles beneath the cathedral-arch aerial roots of the mangroves.

A narrow strip of sandy beach was littered with flotsam and jetsam—pieces of crates probably jettisoned from a passing ship during the storm.

Across several miles of glassy-smooth peacock blue water, a merchant ship leaned unnaturally, stuck fast on the reef.

On Tift's Wharf, the tower lookout spotted the distant wreck—a dot on the horizon through his spyglass—and reached for the bell rope. Clang,

clang, clang, clang! On and on the bell pealed while he shouted "Wreck asho-o-o-ore! Wreck asho-o-o-ore!"

In the Thibodeauxs' parlor, Aaron Matthews, shirtless but clad in his trousers and boots, was asleep on the settee with his arm still encircling the place where Joe had fallen asleep beside him—but she was nowhere in sight. The clanging bell and lookout's cries woke him. He was confused, disoriented, and came to his feet looking around for Joe.

"Good! You're up!"

Aaron, still clearing his head, looked up to see Captain Thibodeaux headed for the front door, buttoning his red jacket as he walked.

"What?" Aaron croaked.

Thibodeaux didn't hesitate. He was already opening the door. "Well, get a move on, boy! We'll need every hand we can get!"

Aaron stood looking at his shirt, rumpled and flattened on the settee where he and Joe had slept on top of it. Dazed, he reached for it and started putting it on.

Alyce Thibodeaux, known in her youth as the Iron Debutante, stopped at the bottom of the stairs, having followed her husband down from their bedroom. She clutched the high ruffled neck of her heavy floor-length dressing gown as she took in Aaron, his rumpled shirt, the settee—and drew her own conclusions. Unyielding disapproval vibrated in her features and her voice.

"You'd better make haste, Mister Matheson."

Captain Thibodeaux called from outside, "Let's go!"

Aaron, dumb as a sheep, turned and followed Thibodeaux out the door.

In the front yard, Aaron was coming alive as he followed the captain toward the front gate, and a thought occurred to him that almost caused him to turn back. *Matheson*?

But there was no turning back. Thibodeaux was striding forward, sucking Aaron along in his wake. Without turning his head, Thibodeaux shouted, "Where away, Josephine Marie?"

From atop the Thibodeaux house, Joe's voice came back: "Alligator Reef!"

Aaron stumbled as he tried to keep pace with Thibodeaux and look up to the rooftop at the same time. "Wha—How did you know she was up th—?" Aaron stammered.

"She's a wrecker's daughter," her father replied without stopping or turning.

In the streets around Tift's Wharf, men and boys of all shapes and sizes came on the run from all corners of Key West, headed for the wrecking sloops in the harbor.

At the intersection of Eaton and Duval Streets the pandemonium increased when a stream of wreckers headed northwest crossed a patrol of Union soldiers headed northeast. The soldiers' destination was the Lowe house on Duval Street, where Caroline's Rebel flag fluttered gaily in the morning breeze.

Until the two groups of men untangled themselves, their growling and whumping and stomping added to the cacophony of bell clanging and lookout shouting. Insults of "Mudsill!" and "Mooncusser!" could be heard from within the swarm.

Aboard the *Lady Alyce* Cataline Simmons, Stepney Austin, and the other crewmen were already in place when Thibodeaux and Aaron boarded the vessel. Sails had been set, all lines but one had been cast off, and the *Lady Alyce* looked ready to plow the waves.

"Cast off, Mister Simmons!" shouted Thibodeaux without breaking stride between dock and boat.

"Aye, sir. Cast off!"

Stepney Austin cast off the one restraining line, and the *Lady Alyce* moved rapidly away.

Thibodeaux boomed, "Stepney Austin!"

"Sir!"

"Get aloft and take a good look toward Alligator Reef!"

Stepney moved to execute the order with primate-like skill.

Aaron stood catching his breath after the race to the wharf. He stretched the kinks from his back and rolled each shoulder, accepting his stiffness as just punishment for foolishly sleeping on a hard, short, grossly uncomfortable settee.

He reached beneath his dangling shirttails to rub the small of his back, and he reacted. The pistol was gone from his waistband. He felt for it. Looked for it. Turned as if to go back for it—but the shoreline was many yards behind and receding fast. Aaron had to work hard to keep the concern from his face as he realized he had a very good idea just where that pistol might be.

An hour later, Lucy Drake was cleaning the Thibodeaux parlor, frowning as she straightened the settee. How did this thing get into such a state? It was askew, rumpled, and even damp. She lifted the white lace antimacassar that had fallen into the seat of the settee, and beneath the lace lay an Army Colt revolver. A Union Army Colt revolver.

Lucy dropped the antimacassar and, picking up the revolver between extended fingers as if it were a live scorpion, she shouted, "Miss Alyce! Miss Alyce, look 'ere!"

At the same time, in the Fort Taylor infirmary, Morgan and the medical officer walked between cots where fevered soldiers lay. An attendant with a bucket of water went from bed to bed, ladling water into the bowl or pitcher at each bedside. Other attendants could be seen sponging water on patients' brows or helping patients to drink.

The two officers were relieved and relatively happy, for once.

"I was like a kid at Christmas," said the medical

officer. "You would have thought it was twenty-dollar gold pieces falling from the heavens. I promised God I'd never take a good storm for granted again. Never."

"Nor I," said Morgan. "As soon as I get the time, I'm taking a long, slow, soak-to-my-eyebrows bath."

The medical officer stopped beside the bed of one of the Pennsylvania farm-boy soldiers who had been patrolling Tift's Wharf on the night Richard Thibodeaux and his friends plotted their escape via the English schooner. The farm boy was delirious with fever, and the medical officer stooped to give him a drink from the bedside pitcher.

The medical officer said, "I mistook my enemy, Colonel. I thought my boys would die under cannon fire or Minié balls. I pictured heathen, slave-flogging Rebels charging with sabers and bayonets. Never, never did I for a moment think that I would see men die because I couldn't get them enough water to ease their fever. Even while sitting on a flyspeck of rock with hundreds of miles of water on every side. I never thought it. Wouldn't have believed it. Never."

"Well, that's over now," Morgan sympathized. "We should have all the water we need for the foreseeable future."

"Maybe not, sir," a voice intruded.

CHAPTER 9

Morgan wheeled to face Sergeant Pfifer, who stood with wet sleeves rolled up and a dripping gunny sack full of something black, wet, and lumpy. The sergeant looked like a man with very bad news.

The fastidious Colonel Morgan was offended by Pfifer's disheveled, filthy appearance. "How dare you come in here looking like—Great Scott, Sergeant! What an ungodly smell! Get that out of here!"

The sergeant, not intimidated, insisted, "I thought the doctor should know right away, sir. Someone apparently got into our cistern early this morning and contaminated the water supply."

"What!" The shocked medical officer stood abruptly.

"Contaminated! With that?" said Morgan, eyeing the reeking sack in the sergeant's fist.

"Yes, sir."

"What is it?" asked the medical officer.

"Rats, sir. Stinkin' dead rats."

On the bed, the delirious farm boy rolled his head and moaned, "Rats. These pirate ships are full of them."

Morgan looked grim. "Apparently one of them isn't. Not any longer."

On the southern ramparts of the fort, two Union sentries stood lazily at their posts in the blazing sun. One, a sharpshooter, was putting a percussion cap on his muzzle-loader. The other sentry watched idly, musing, "Wish I knew where I could get fifty dollars. I'd sure admire to have one of them Henry repeaters. Sixteen shots without stopping to reload."

"You can get off three rounds a minute with one of these if you know your business," the sharpshooter bragged. "I reckon we could win this war killin' three Rebs a minute. Besides, you and me ain't never gonna see no fifty dollars all in one place."

The sentry turned to gaze out over the ramparts toward the untamed jungle that was 80 percent of the island. His own muzzle-loader hung limp in its strap from his shoulder. He fished a bandanna out of his pocket and wiped sweat from his face and neck.

"You ain't never gonna kill three Rebs a minute on Key West, neither," he told the sharpshooter. "Three pelicans a minute, maybe, but pelicans ain't likely to win the war nohow. Bet you can't hit that one."

He pointed to a pelican gliding over the ocean 150 yards offshore.

The sharpshooter, his reputation at stake, took careful aim and boomed off a shot.

The sentry was impressed. "Got him! I swear, boy, you still got the touch!"

The sharpshooter looked at the sky overhead and horror crossed his features. He yanked the rifle from the sentry's shoulder and stuffed his own empty gun into the sentry's gut, saying, "Load this!"

The sharpshooter took aim at something in the sky. The surprised sentry fumbled the empty rifle then automatically reached into his cartridge pouch for a cartridge and talked as he bit off the cartridge end and poured power and shot down the muzzle of the gun. It seemed to be taking forever to load.

"What is it? What's going on!" the sentry gasped.

The sharpshooter squinted and pulled the trigger of the sentry's rifle, and it clacked—a misfire. The sentry, wide-eyed and flushed, was ramming the barrel of the gun he was loading.

"Dang!" the sharpshooter yelled. "He's getting away! Hurry up!" He snatched the rifle away before the sentry could replace the ramrod in its rack. The sharpshooter dug in his pouch for a percussion cap and slapped it into place, trying not to take his eyes off the sky where he had been aiming.

The sentry was left holding his own misfired gun and the ramrod from the sharpshooter's gun, and he was frightened and bewildered. "Who's getting away?" He looked skyward, following the barrel of the rifle now aimed by the sharpshooter, and there, now far distant, a carrier pigeon wended its way toward the open sea. It was headed straight for Cuba.

The sharpshooter squinted, pulled the trigger, the rifle boomed—and both soldiers stood motionless, not even breathing, looking at the sky. Hopeless doom clouded their faces.

The sentry mumbled almost inaudibly, "Yessir, I'd sure admire to have one of them Henry repeaters."

"Shut up," said the sharpshooter. "You and your pelicans!"

That evening on Tift's Wharf, a hard day's work had ended, and the wrecking fleet rode at anchor in Key West harbor once more.

Cataline Simmons and Aaron Matthews had stayed behind to finish coiling the lines, battening the hatches, and making the *Lady Alyce* shipshape. In the background, all over the harbor, other wreckers were doing the same. In the streets men were walking homeward, exhausted.

Cataline stood back from closing the last hatch and stretched his bulky muscles. He moved toward the gunwale, to step from the boat to the dock, saying to Aaron, "You're a good seaman."

Aaron looked up from the neat coil of line he had just finished. "Comes from a great desire to leave home, coupled with a great lack of money."

Cataline smiled at this. "I've worked my way to a

place or two in my time. Some learn slow, some learn fast, but we all learn if we live. The sea is a stern tutor. I'm grateful for your help today. Without Richard,..." He left the thought unfinished.

Aaron stepped off the boat to join Cataline on the dock. They began to walk toward home.

"That reminds me," Aaron said, remembering the night of Richard's departure and the unknown setter of a false light, "I need to talk to a man named Cornish. Know him?"

"Everyone knows Sandy Cornish. Strongest man on the island. Something big needs moving, people get six boys together to move it, or they get Sandy Cornish. Cheaper to get Sandy Cornish."

Aaron digested this information. "So, you think I should try not to make him mad."

Cataline grinned. "I figured you for a fast learner."

At William Curry's store it was closing time, and the only person in the room other than Curry himself was Colonel Morgan. Morgan was not shopping, however. He was dressed to the nines for a fancy dinner party at the home of a wealthy Conch, and he stood by the door, slapping his empty gloves against his palm. "Well, when you do see him," Morgan told Curry, "be good enough to tell him I want him in my quarters at midnight tonight. Tonight, understand?"

Curry looked through the storefront window and, outside on the street, Cataline and Aaron could be seen walking together.

"There he is, not fifty feet from you at this very minute. Why don't you tell him yourself?"

Morgan glanced out but turned angry eyes back upon Curry. "I can't be seen talking to the man on the street, you idiot, and I am already late to escort Miss Dauthier to a social engagement. You see to it. It's your job."

Morgan exited, slamming the shop door behind him. Curry looked with distaste at the closed door. "Aye," he muttered, "and what, may I ask, is your job, Mister Morgan, sir?"

Dusk was deepening from rose to gray when Cataline and Aaron arrived at the front gate of a small, neat shack set back behind a lush, well-tended garden and a hand-built fence of coquina rock with bromeliads and coconuts sprouting in its crevices. Cataline gestured to Aaron that this was the place and started to walk away.

"You're not coming in?" Aaron asked.

"I'll see you tomorrow, maybe." Cataline walked away.

Aaron looked after him, worried. "'Maybe'?"

CHAPTER 10

Aaron rapped his knuckles on the heavy wooden door and turned to admire the garden. When the door opened, Aaron turned back with his mouth open to greet Sandy Cornish—but there was only empty air where Aaron was looking. He adjusted downward and there, spindly and shy, was a 9-year-old slave child.

"Oh, hello," he said with a bow. "Ah, I'm looking for Mister Cornish. Ah, do you...?"

"I'm Sandy Cornish." The door swung wider, driven by the rake-like hand of a large black man over 70 years old. The man gave Aaron a suspicious look then gently urged the child out the door with his other huge hand. "You get on home now, Salina. Tell your missy I'll be there first thing tomorrow to see to her papayas."

The timid child slipped past Aaron and disappeared toward Sandy's front gate. Sandy gestured Aaron into the one-room house, that seemed even smaller with such a big man standing in it. "Too much rain all at once sometimes," said Cornish. "Bad for papaya trees."

"My name is Matthews. I—"

"You come in the *St. Gertrude.*" Cornish sat down in a home-built rocking chair that rested on a rag rug next to a hand-hewn table where an oil lamp glowed. He took up a whetstone and a wicked-looking machete from the floor beside his chair and continued what he had been doing before Aaron arrived: putting a razor edge on the machete's blade.

"Yes, well, that's true, yes, but that doesn't have anything to do with why I'm here. I—"

"You need somethin' moved?"

"No, I, thank you, no, I don't need anything moved. What I need is information, really. Something you might know, something you could tell me that would help me."

"Help you what?"

"Send messages to Havana, maybe." Aaron almost held his breath pending Cornish's answer.

"I don't do no marketing in Havana no more. Too hard to get back and forth these days. I sell enough produce right here in Key West. I don't need no trouble. I get by."

"Yes, I'm sure you do," Aaron said cheerily. "That's a wonderful garden, by the way. Beautiful. Just beautiful. Really. They told me to look for the best vegetable garden in town if I wanted to find Sandy Cornish, and by golly, they were right.

Wonderful. Really."

Cornish put down his whetstone and, the machete dangling in one hand, stood up from his chair and towered over his visitor. "You don't want no vegetables."

"Ah, no. No, that's exactly right, I don't. I, ah, I'm interested in birds, actually."

"Sold my birds. Like I said, I don't do business in Cuba no more. No sense keeping no pigeons. Got no messages to send."

Aaron felt he was close to getting the information he sought, and the feeling made him bold. Perhaps too bold.

"Did you sell your birds to Noah Lewis?" Aaron asked pointedly.

An instant later the front door slammed open and Aaron Matthews flew out of it, tumbled down the rickety wooden steps, and sprawled full-length on the garden path.

Sandy Cornish, having tossed Aaron out, cast a long shadow as he stood solidly in the doorway, lamplight pouring from behind him. "Mister, you got business with me, fine. You want to *meddle* in my business, I ain't got time for ya. You want to talk Noah Lewis's business, you talk to Noah Lewis."

Cornish stomped back into the house and the door whapped shut.

Aaron raised himself slowly from the ground, rubbing his new bruises. "Thanks," he murmured. "I will."

After midnight, Colonel Morgan's quarters were dark. The lock clanked, keys jangled, hinges creaked, and Morgan's uniform rustled in the blackness. His boots scraped and clomped as he entered. A match flared. Morgan lit the oil lamp on the table. His dress finery flashed and gleamed in the yellow light. He began to remove shiny accessories, humming like a man pleased with himself.

"You're late," came out of the darkness.

Morgan did not look up from his undressing. "Good of you to come. We could have used you earlier today, but of course you had gone sailing."

Aaron emerged from a chair in the darkest corner of the room. He still wore the clothing he had slept in the night before—but he had at least tucked in his shirttail.

Morgan continued, "I will not ask how you got in here. 'Set a thief to catch a thief,' isn't that what they say?"

"I'm no thief."

Morgan clearly disagrees. "While you were at the pirate regatta this morning, your Rebel friend was busy poisoning my cisterns. Tell me, was there enough loot to make it worth the lives of the men who may die because of it?"

Aaron grabbed Morgan's shoulder and jerked him around, forcing him to talk face-to-face. Aaron's knuckles whitened as his fist clenched around Morgan's lapel.

"They are not 'pirates,'" Aaron enunciated carefully. "They are people. Just like you. Just like me. Just people. And there was no 'loot' because a pigheaded Connecticut Yankee of a captain who believes everything he hears decided not to let the evil 'mooncussers' aboard his beloved ship until it was too late. These people risked their lives and their boats to save nothing more than the miserable skins of the captain and crew—for which there will be no charge, thank you."

Disgusted, Aaron shoved Morgan backward a step and released his lapel. "If men die from bad water in the cisterns of Fort Zachary Taylor, it won't be because I put to sea this morning; it will be because they are soldiers and we, like it or not, are at war! And I'm not here to 'catch a thief,' I'm here to find a spy and a saboteur so we can end the dying—from bad water or anything else!"

Morgan, unrepentant, straightened his clothing where Aaron had rumpled it. "Well, when you find him," said Morgan, "you might ask him what he told the Rebel Navy in today's message."

"Today's—! But your man—!"

"He missed."

Aaron threw up his hands, turned his back on Morgan, and slumped into the chair in the corner once more. He was only a voice in the darkness when he said, "Dear God, what next?"

Morgan resumed undressing, a man obsessed with his regalia of office and his own importance. "I'll tell you what's next. One of two alternatives. Either you bring me the man who poisoned my water and wants to set the Rebel Navy upon me at my weakest moment, or I assume that every citizen of Key West is potentially that man, and I deal with them all."

"What, hang them all?" Aaron scoffed. "A whole town of innocent people? You'd be court martialed, or worse."

"One of these people is far from innocent, Lieutenant. I intend to hang that one from the highest point in this fort while this fort is still in Union hands. And if you do not find that one for me, the fate of all the others is on your head."

Aaron bolted out of the chair and across the room to the door. With his back to Morgan, he ground out, "I won't listen to any more of this. Goodnight. ... *Sir.*"

"Miss Dauthier sends you her regards, by the way," Morgan said.

"You told her you'd be seeing me!"

"She rather assumed it, I think. I am pleased to see you've taken my advice and quit carrying a firearm."

Aaron touched the small of his back, where his pistol used to reside. He hesitated as if he would say something about it, but decided against it and, in silence, left the room.

Upon reaching the Thibodeaux house, Aaron slipped quietly in at the front door and looked around. He was alone. He felt his way to the settee and poked around and beneath it, searching for his pistol. No luck. He looked toward the upper floors, made a decision, and headed for the stairs.

He arrived at the top of the stairs and slunk to a bedroom door. Light glowed under the door from a lamp burning on the other side. Aaron pressed himself flat against the door. "Joe!" he whispered. "Joe, are you awake?"

"Come in," a voice whispered from beyond the door.

Aaron eased the door open, slipped in, and turned his back to the room to close the door quietly. He stiffened. The cold metal barrel of a gun was poking him in the middle of his back.

"Is this what you were looking for, Mister Matheson?" she said.

CHAPTER 11

Aaron recognized the voice but dared not turn to look. "You mistake me for someone else, Miz Alyce," he said. "Matthews is the name."

"The only person I might mistake you for, Aaron Burgess Matheson, is your father when he was thirty years younger. You have your mother's eyes, though. You may turn around ... slowly. I am an excellent shot, by the way."

Aaron turned very carefully to face her, and she backed up out of his reach, still pointing the gun at his middle.

"I don't understand," he said.

"Of course you do. Charleston. We all used to be back and forth almost every month, before the war—visiting and shopping. I was at the very cotillion where your mother met your father. I know very well who—and what—you are."

Aaron looked around the room as if expecting

Joe to step out of a shadow at any moment.

"She is not here," Alyce said. "A neighbor with a sick baby. I sent Joe over there with our milk goat. She'll stay the night."

"Away from me," he said.

"Very much away from you," she agreed.

Aaron leaned back against the bedroom door, taking in all the ramifications of what Alyce had told him. Alyce, deadly calm, kept the pistol leveled at his chest.

"Does anyone else know who I am?" Aaron asked.

"I don't know. *I* didn't tell them."

Silently they studied one another. Alyce put the pistol down on the dresser and folded her arms. "Did you know your brother joined the army? The Confederate Army?" she asked.

Aaron nodded, a bit sadly.

"Do your parents even know if you are alive or dead?" Alyce asked.

"I don't know. *I* didn't tell them."

They exchanged a wry smile.

Alyce's eyes changed as she looked into the past. "I haven't seen Melinda Burgess since we were girls." Then she pulled herself back to the loathsome present. "Wouldn't it be ironic if Richard and your brother became friends in the army! We can all laugh about it when they come home." She paused. "Please, God."

"Amen," said Aaron.

Alyce picked up the pistol and brought it to him,

pressing it into his hands, and stepped back. "You will stay away from Josephine Marie, Mister Matheson."

"And if I can't do that?"

"Then you will become porch gossip: 'a Yankee spy from a good family in Charleston, isn't it sad?' And one morning they'll find your body on Tift's Wharf with a sailor's bootknife where your heart should be."

"Whose knife?" said Aaron. "Yours?"

Alyce nearly smiled. "In the most southern city in the country? Practically anyone's."

Aboard the Rebel ship anchored in Havana harbor that same night, the commanding officer stood beside his desk watching his executive officer decode a message.

Javi, the bird handler, fidgeted nervously just inside the closed cabin door. "I know you want fast," said Javi, "and your man he already come and go for today. I know you don't want Javi wait for tomorrow."

"No, you did exactly right, Javi," the C.O. said. "You did well. Why don't you go now and tell the deck officer I said you deserve a bottle for your trouble, eh?"

Javi smiled his snaggle-toothed, lopsided smile and, bowing like a grateful peon, backed quietly out the door.

The Rebel X.O. finished writing out the decoded message and handed it to the commander.

The commander read the message, and what he read seemed to make him happy. "Things are not going well at Fort Taylor," he said. "We must pay them a visit very soon."

"We're still outnumbered and outgunned by the Union's Caribbean fleet," said the Exec.

"Yes, well, that's where our representative in Key West will be the biggest help of all. What is the one thing Key West Conchs do better than anyone else?"

The Rebel X.O. thinks for a second, and his smile widens to match that of his commander. "They wreck ships."

"Exactly. See if Javi has left the ship. I need to send a bird to Key West first thing in the morning."

In the same night, at the White House, President Lincoln stood in his dressing gown, reading a dispatch while his adviser watched him excitedly.

"I'm sorry to wake you, sir," the adviser nearly burbled in excitement, "but this is what we've been waiting for, isn't it? Well, not exactly the great victory we would have hoped, I know, but we can't help it if McClellan was too stu—, I mean, it's too late now to say we should have pursued them and finished them off. You said even a stalemate—and this is a little better than that. No one can say we actually lost."

Lincoln was grim. "Over twelve thousand of our boys might tell you they lost something at Antietam Creek, if you could talk to them without requiring the services of a medium."

The adviser looked almost ashamed of himself for a second, but he overcame it and, touching the president's elbow, ushered him toward his desk. "We can't let their sacrifice be in vain," the adviser said. "They have bought us the advantage we needed. Now is the time. Sign it now. Tonight. And by tomorrow the news will be on its way around the world."

The president nodded wearily, sat down at the desk, and reached for a pen. The adviser eagerly shoved a prepared document in front of President Lincoln for his signature.

At dawn, Joe Thibodeaux bounded down the stairs from her bedroom and knocked a soft, quick tattoo on Aaron's door. She looked upstairs to be sure no one had taken notice. She smiled, anticipating a happy welcome.

The door opened a crack, the turtling stick was thrust out at her, and the door closed. Joe deflated a little but, still optimistic, refused to give up. "Aaron," she whispered. No answer. "Aaron! Open this door!"

She heard the lock shifting, felt the knob turn, and she pushed her way inside.

Aaron backed quickly away from the door and from any contact with Joe. Fully dressed, he was stiff and aloof. The bed was loosely made, as if someone had sat or lain upon it but hadn't slept.

Joe, hurt and confused, stopped moving toward

him when he retreated. "What's the matter with you?"

"Nothing's the matter. I'm ... busy, that's all."

"Busy! It's hardly light yet. What can you possibly be busy at?"

He fidgeted and looked at the floor. He couldn't give her an answer.

Joe watched him, wanting him to have an explanation and disappointed when he didn't. Pain showed in her eyes. "I'm sorry," she murmured. "I thought ... I thought you liked me."

Aaron caught himself when he nearly moved involuntarily toward her. "You, of all people, should've smelled a wreck coming," he said.

This stung her, but she fought to keep up a good front and bluff her way through. "Well, all right. We'll change course," she said. She swallowed hard.

Aaron kept a stone facade, but he wanted nothing more than to crawl under a rock and shrivel.

"Friends?" Joe said.

He nodded lamely.

"Want to go turtling?" she offered.

"No. I have to see a man about a bird."

"Arnau?"

Aaron shook his head. "Another man. Noah Lewis."

Joe brightened a bit, seeing a way to stay close to him. "You don't know anybody in the colored quarter. You'll never find him. I better go with you."

"No!" he said, too quickly. Then more slowly he added, "No, it wouldn't do your reputation any good to be seen waltzing through the colored quarter with a known reprobate like me. I'll find him."

She could see it, hard, cold, and undeniable. He was sending her away, and not just for this morning. He couldn't mean it. "You ... you're sure?" Joe asked.

From downstairs came a shout of, "Josephine Marie! Where are you!"

Aaron reacted to the sound of Alyce Thibodeaux's voice. He nervously rubbed his chest. He was sure now. "Cross my heart and hope to die," he said, trying to keep any trace of gentleness from his voice. "You go on now."

With a last wistful look in his direction, Joe slipped out the door.

Aaron, hand over his heart, let out a sigh as if he had been holding his breath for a week.

...

At a Union Navy outpost on Jamaica, a carriage pulled up in front of a house that had been hastily converted to military use. A uniformed officer carrying a mail pouch dismounted from the carriage and entered the house.

A large parlor had been arranged into an office. The uniformed officer removed papers from his pouch onto a desk and accepted papers to insert into his pouch from the yeoman seated there. A Yankee executive officer approached the broadest desk in the room with a handful of papers from the incoming pouch.

The X.O. handed one of the papers to the

commanding officer working at the broad desk. "He's done it, sir," the X.O. said. "Effective January first."

The Yankee C.O. read the document then leaned back in his chair. "Well, well, well, well," he murmured. Then he raised his voice to address everyone in the room: "Gentlemen, it appears we are now the champions of freedom for men of all colors. Effective January first, eighteen sixty-three, all slaves in the southern states are declared free by order of President Abraham Lincoln."

Comments of acknowledgment and approval rumbled through the room, then every man returned to his task. The executive officer, with other papers in hand, remained at the C.O.'s desk. "Does this mean the English won't officially recognize the Confederacy, sir?"

The C.O. responded, "So long as the Secesh don't do something spectacular—which we will do our best to prevent." He held out his hand toward the additional papers. "What else do you have there?"

The X.O. dealt the rest of his papers onto the desk as he enumerated them: "Intelligence reports possible Rebel ships massing in Havana, Cuba—if a number that small can be termed a 'mass'—;" he set out another paper, "copy of orders being delivered simultaneously to the commanding officer at Fort Zachary Taylor—;" then he set out the last paper from the pouch, "sealed orders for your eyes only, sir."

The commanding officer opened this last and scanned the page quickly.

The executive officer stood by, curious.

The commandant handed the X.O. the orders to read for himself and stood up to say to the room, “Lay on supplies and fresh water, gentlemen. We’re going to Key West.”

CHAPTER 12

Inside Noah Lewis's shack, birds cooed and rustled. Aaron Matthews emerged from the tropical greenery running rampant around the sun-bleached building and knocked on the door. No answer.

"Noah Lewis?" Aaron knocked harder, and the door swung away from him. He looked, but there was no person opening it. He pushed the door open wider. "Noah Lewis?"

On the floor beside a wall of pigeon cages lay a black man with a knife hilt protruding from a blood-soaked shirtfront.

"Noah—," Aaron began. A shadow crossed his back. An object slammed into the back of Aaron's head with a solid thwump he never even heard. Aaron Matthews dropped like an anchor, unconscious.

It was only mid-afternoon, and William Curry appeared agitated as he shoved a "Closed" sign into the window and hastily drew the shades. Then he retreated to the back of his store.

Curry bustled to where Aaron Matthews sat slumped miserably over a cluttered desk—Curry's own. Aaron was conscious, but he looked like everything including his hair and eyelashes were hurting.

"I don't know how you made it here without being seen," said Curry, skittering about the room.

"I wouldn't have if Sandy hadn't come along with that produce cart," Aaron said.

The hulking Sandy Cornish entered through Curry's back door with a bucket of water. "You lucky that no-account owed me money, else I wouldn't go nowhere near Noah Lewis's place. No tellin' who mighta found you, or when. What you want with trash like Noah?"

Sandy produced a cloth from a deep pocket in his mammoth trousers and, using the freshly drawn water, made a cool compress, which he applied to the back of Aaron's head.

Aaron inhaled sharply in pain then closed his eyes against it. "I wanted to talk to him about some work he did a while back. His employer obviously didn't want him discussing it."

"You're sure Lewis was dead?" Curry asked.

Aaron opened one eye to answer that question with a look.

Sandy Cornish fished in another pocket and produced the bloody knife. He showed it to Curry. "Found this right where his heart woulda been, if Noah Lewis ever had one."

"Bootknife," murmured Curry.

Aaron's eyes zapped open. "What?"

"It's a bootknife," Curry repeated. "An old one. Seen some use. Probably a sailor or a sponger. Turtler maybe."

Aaron suddenly had a bad taste in his mouth. "You sell a lot of these?" he asked.

"Aye, plenty," said the Scotsman. "Sold one to Joe Thibodeaux just yesterday—said hers come up missing. Real sad about it she was. It was a present from Richard, before he went to soldiering."

Aaron's eyes closed. He let his head drop onto his chest and motioned Sandy's ministering hands away. "I don't want to hear any more."

Curry gave Sandy a look, and Sandy picked up his bucket and left.

Curry took a deep breath. "Then I'm sorry to say there's more I'm bound to tell ya. You've got a meeting to go to tonight."

...

The sunset drenched the mangroves along Key West's southern shore with incomparable colors. Colonel Morgan lounged in the shadow of a jagged brick wall—one side of a Martello Tower still under construction. The distant horizon was awash in oranges, pinks, blues, and greens where the sky met the sea, but Morgan was ignoring it—polishing his buttons with his cuff.

Out of the shadows a hand clamped down firmly on Morgan's shoulder, scaring him out of his wits. "Matthews?"

"Who else would be looking for you in this vermin-infested swamp, Morgan?"

"Did you find the Rebel spy's hired man?"

Aaron eased into a clear spot and squatted down, almost invisible in the tangled vegetation and lengthening shadows. "Yes, I found him."

"Well? What did he say? Who paid him?"

"He was dead when I got there."

"Dead? Murdered, you mean."

Aaron nodded, watching the sunset, tracing shapes in the sand with one finger.

Morgan ruminated on the news, or lack of it. Then he roused himself to full height and full purpose. "Then you can't deliver the Rebel saboteur as we'd hoped."

"Even a dead man can say a lot, of you know how to listen," Aaron said.

"Spare me your riddles, Lieutenant. If you have something to report, I want to hear it. If not, as I've told you before, I plan to take drastic action."

Aaron fixed Morgan with his eyes for the first time this night. "You make a lot of noise about hanging the man from the highest point in the fort, Morgan. But what if it isn't a man? What if it's a boy, barely more than a child? Or even a woman? What would you do then? Send her to prison at Fort Jefferson? Toss her in the brig at Fort Taylor and try to keep your own men away from her for the remainder of the war? What?"

"Who is it?"

"Just answer the question."

"What's good for the goose is good for the gander. A rope is a rope, and a spy is a spy. Who is it?"

Aaron stared at Morgan a moment longer then dropped his eyes to the sand and drew a deep breath. He looked again at the horizon, but the sun had disappeared now. "I don't know," Aaron said. "But I'm close. Real close."

Morgan produced a folded paper from within his tunic and poked it at Aaron. Aaron lit a match to read it. The yellow waves of matchlight cast eerie shadows through the hoopskirt mangrove roots.

"Close isn't good enough," said Morgan. "I will not expose the entire Gulf of Mexico to the Rebel Navy because you are incapable of accomplishing your mission."

Aaron read from the folded paper, " '... immediately send to Port Royal post the families (white) of all persons who have husbands, brothers, or sons in Rebel employment ... or who have uttered any disloyal word....' " He looked at Morgan. "You're not seriously thinking of applying these ridiculous standards here!"

"I have my orders—or rather, Colonel Good's orders—and while he is in South Carolina, I intend to carry them out."

"You'll use this excuse to decimate the population of the entire island!" Aaron cried.

Morgan was grim. "And send them to starve alongside the Southern Army in its decrepit camps in the dead of winter."

Aaron handed the dispatch back to the colonel. “For the love of mercy,” Aaron pleaded, “send them to Nassau, or Green Turtle Cay, or ... or Havana. Places they know. Where they have family, friends, a chance....”

“You were their chance, Lieutenant. All I want is the one who is a danger to me, to my command. And I will have him, one way or another. And don’t think you can simply refuse to obey my orders. A dozen of my officers have already tried that, and they are all sweltering in the brig now and for the foreseeable future.”

Aaron stood and turned toward Morgan in the deepening dark. Morgan could not see Aaron’s face, but his posture telegraphed the threat that was no doubt burning in his eyes.

Morgan braced himself for a blow, but none came. Only a quiet, carefully controlled voice.

“How much time do I have?”

...

The next day a crowd gathered on Tift’s Wharf as Sergeant Pfifer tacked up a placard:

“EVACUATION ORDER”

“By Command of Maj. Gen. D. Hunter, Headquarters, Department of the South, Hilton Head, Port Royal, South Carolina, January 29, 1863:”

The remainder of the notice was obscured by the crowd, but the reactions of everyone on the wharf indicated disaster.

Joseph Porter, Josephine Marie Thibodeaux, and the remaining Conch boys who had attended the midnight meetings at Tift's warehouse, gathered in a knot, aghast at the placard, and whispered to one another.

Caroline Lowe and her mother pushed their way to the front of the crowd to read the placard.

"They can't mean this, Sergeant!"

" 'Fraid so, Miss Caroline," answered Pfifer.

"But to turn us out of our homes!" cried Mrs. Lowe. "To leave us with nothing! In exile!"

The sergeant gave Caroline a meaningful look and spared a glance to the roof of Lowe house, where Caroline's Rebel flag usually flew. "Maybe if you just hadn't kept things stirred up all the time," he said.

From the fringe of the crowd, Aaron Matthews watched Joe Thibodeaux to the exclusion of all else. He made a decision and began working his way through the crowd toward her. The group of Rebel boys parted grudgingly for him, reluctant to give up one of their own to a relative stranger, but at last he stood before Josephine Marie.

She looked at him with pain in her eyes but said nothing and made no move toward him.

"I've got to talk to you," he began, "I—"

"Good day, Mister Matthews," snapped Alyce Thibodeaux, swooping between them like a mother eagle protecting the nest. Alyce took her daughter's arm and pulled Joe away through the crowd. "If you'll excuse us," Alyce shouted over her shoulder, "we have belongings to dispose of and only a few days to do it."

The group of boys closed between Aaron and the departing women, effectively preventing him from following.

Aaron gave up and turned away.

CHAPTER 13

Colonel Morgan and Lila Dauthier strolled arm-in-arm along the breezy upper level of the ramparts of Fort Taylor. Lila laughed and leaned against him, and he puffed up like a grouse in a mating dance.

"I swear, Colonel, you are so droll," Lila fawned. "And I feel guilty being so gay while everyone in town is depressed about that horrible evacuation."

"Don't trouble your pretty head about that, Miss Dauthier," he replied. "Neither you nor any other loyal National need have any fear with regard to that order. Only those whose sympathies are with the rebellion will suffer, and that is as it should be."

Their stroll took them to the eastern end of the ramparts, where a sentry and sharpshooter stood at their posts. Oddly, the two men had laid out a conspicuous row of half a dozen muzzle-loaders, primed and ready, leaning neatly against the brick wall beside them. The two soldiers, each with his gun in hand, stood alert and straining their eyes skyward. Today they would not miss anything that dared fly past them.

Lila took in this strange tableau as Colonel Morgan ushered her down the steps toward the parade ground.

Meanwhile, on a Jamaican mountaintop, the Yankee executive officer stood looking eastward across the Caribbean when his commanding officer, accompanied by a young ensign, stepped up from behind him.

Below in the harbor the U.S. ships stood ready to leave for Key West.

"Well," said the C.O., "I confess I feel naked sailing without the mortars and a few of the cannon, but our job is not to shell the fort, is it."

"No, sir," the Exec said. "I wish you'd reconsider the timing, sir. Sailing the Florida Straits at night is a risky business."

"Yes, but you will keep us off the reefs, won't you, Ensign?" asked the C.O., turning toward the younger man.

"Aye, aye, sir!"

"Good. I wouldn't want to be rescued by the very people I'm expected to carry away." The C.O. returned his attention to the Exec. "What are you looking at?"

The X.O. gestured to the northern horizon, where a dim line of mountaintops could barely be seen on this clear day. "Cuba," he said. "Where they are. Between us and Key West. We're stripped down to carry passengers, and we've got to cross Johnny Reb's doorstep to get where we're going. Respectfully, sir ... I don't like it much."

The C.O. put an arm on the Exec's shoulder and turned him around, walking him back down the hill. The ensign gave a concerned look at the mountaintops on the horizon before following them.

"Relax, my friend," the C.O. was saying. "We'll slip by like a black cat in the dark. The Reb Navy will never even know we were there."

However, at the same time, aboard the Rebel ship in Havana harbor, the Confederate naval commander at his desk was handed a message by his executive officer, who had just decoded it.

"They're coming," said the Southern Exec. "We've got 'em."

The commander read the message, gathered his thoughts, and gave his orders: "Have the decks whitewashed. I want to be able to find our equipment in the dark. I want extra water barrels on the deck for fire-fighting and drinking, and I want all extra chains hung on the gunwales of the steamers to protect the machinery from cannon fire."

"Aye, sir."

"Let's put a spare hawser in the stern of each ship, in case someone needs a tow, and I want a mortar on the deck of every schooner. When we get close enough, we'll lob some shot over the walls of Fort Taylor."

The executive officer rose and went to the door to relay these orders but stopped for one last concern. "We're still outnumbered, sir."

"We won't be after we've run a few of them onto the reefs," the C.O. replied.

On Key West, Aaron Matthews was pacing the beach, turning over and over in his hands the bootknife belonging to a murderer. He felt like a man being eaten by barracuda from the inside out. His suspicions as to the knife's ownership were as strong as they were unacceptable. Anchor chains weighed on both sides of his soul, forcing him first in one direction and then in another. He had a job to do. He had a friend to save. He had a war to end. He had a heart to protect. All seemed the right things to do, but only half his options were possible, the exercising of one "duty" resulting in the destruction of the other.

The tension built in him as if a metal spring were being wound more and more tightly. Aaron whirled suddenly and zinged the knife—whap!—into a tree. His emotional spring had snapped.

Atop Fort Taylor, the sentry and sharpshooter stood alongside their makeshift arsenal and strained their eyes toward different quadrants of the sky.

Suddenly the sharpshooter jerked himself taller, whipped his gun to his shoulder, and boomed a shot at the sky. The sentry spun around. The sharpshooter turned to look at the sentry, and a proud grin spread across his face. He nodded smartly. *Got him this time!*

...

That night in Morgan's quarters, Aaron worked at Morgan's desk, decoding a message, while Morgan waited impatiently. Aaron finished writing out the message and sat back in the chair staring at it. Silent.

"Well?" said Morgan.

Aaron was deep in thought. He heard nothing.

Morgan stepped to the desk and snatched up the transcription to read for himself. "What is he telling them this time?"

Aaron reached up and took the paper out of Morgan's hands.

Morgan had read the opening words of it, however. "It's to you!" Morgan cried.

"Apparently."

"And extremely ... personal ... in nature, it would seem! This is from a woman!"

Aaron folded the transcription and poked it behind his belt buckle. "It would seem so. And she knows enough about your operation to be fairly sure the message would be intercepted by you and handed to me. We are both found out, Colonel."

Morgan grabbed the much-creased coded legband message from the desk where Aaron had been working on it. He shook it before Aaron's face and took a deep breath. "She ... they ... know about the fleet coming here from Jamaica for the evacuation. I infer there is some plan to ambush our ships en route and, following that, to attack Fort

Taylor and reclaim Key West for the Confederacy.

"They could turn the tide of the entire war," Morgan concluded. He waited for a response from Aaron, but none seemed forthcoming. "Well, is that all?"

"No."

"Let's have it, Lieutenant."

"The lady implies that she and I ... that we have known one another well."

"Romantically, you mean."

"Yes, sir."

"Surely this narrows down the suspects, even for you. Who is it, then?"

"I ... can't say, sir."

Morgan looked at him with disgust. "No, of course not. Your reputation as a womanizer is well founded, isn't it. By linking her to you we've limited our list of possibilities to a mere census of the females alive on the island." Morgan shook the original message in front of Aaron's face again. "Well, what do you make of this signature, then? This ... drawing of something. What is it? A dove?"

He showed the simple line drawing of a bird at the bottom of the message to Aaron, as if Aaron needed a reminder.

"Probably a carrier pigeon," Aaron said. "That would be the obvious connection, wouldn't it?"

Morgan crushed the paper in his fist and slumped into the nearest chair. "Nothing is obvious to me any more."

Aaron rested his elbows on the colonel's desk

and dropped his head into his hands. He would do his job because he must, to save his brother. But if he did his job, would he be able to save Josephine Marie? Or at least save her family?

After a moment, he lifted his head, ran a hand through his hair, and stood up to face Morgan. "If I can promise you I'll stop her, that no harm will come to the fleet or the fort because of her, will you cancel the evacuation of these innocent people?"

Morgan, slouched in his chair, was incredulous. "On your word alone? Are you insane? What have you ever been but a reckless wastrel, Matthews? When did your promise ever mean anything to anybody? No, I know you too well to cancel the evacuation order based on anything you might promise me."

"Then I respectfully request permission to send a message to Colonel Good in South Carolina immediately, sir."

Morgan oozed up from his chair to face Aaron with every ounce of superiority he could muster. "Send your message, Lieutenant. It won't change a thing. Colonel Good knows you even better than I do."

"I'm counting on that, sir."

...

It was a busy day on Key West. At Lowe house, Caroline and Bianca Lowe, with the help of Bogy Sands, buried their valuables in the back yard.

William Curry and his wife, Euphemie, were taking merchandise off the shelves and packing it away in boxes for storage. Aaron Matthews entered the store, looked around, and seemed surprised to find it empty of customers and almost empty of merchandise. "William! Not you, too!" No one knew better than Aaron how loyal William Curry had been to the Federals.

"My wife's brother, Albert, was one of the boys who went with Richard Thibodeaux and the others," Curry explained.

Without looking up from her work, Euphemie commented, "And my sister, Caroline, has made it her business to antagonize the mudsills ever since."

Curry was genuinely shocked. "Euphemie! Such language! 'Mudsills' indeed." He looked at Aaron and continued, "I'm sorry."

"No, William, I'm sorry," said Aaron. Uncomfortable and ashamed, he left the Currys to their packing.

In the Thibodeaux back yard, Alyce and Lucy were wrapping silverware in oilskins and dropping it into the cistern. Aaron came through the gate without passing through the house. Alyce saw him. "Lucy, go and get the rest of the flatware out of the buffet, please," Alyce said.

Lucy looked at Alyce, then at Aaron, then went without comment into the house.

Aaron advanced to where Alyce was sitting and lowered himself into the place Lucy had vacated. He began to help wrap the ornate monogrammed silverware.

Alyce held up a piece and examined the handle.

It bore the initial "G." Alyce smiled wryly and said, "I don't suppose there's a family in town that has its own initials on the silverware. With the possible exception of Will and Euphemie Curry, naturally."

Aaron smiled and nodded. Most of the luxuries enjoyed by Key West Conchs were the spoils of wrecked ships bound for other families' homes, in faraway cities.

"You'll have the house to yourself after we're gone," said Alyce. "I've asked Lucy to come in to clean for you, but I'm afraid she doesn't like you much. Technically, she is a free woman now. It would be nice if you could pay her wages—especially since they can be paid to her now, instead of to Mr. Dennis."

"Yes, ma'am."

They continued in silence for a moment, each wrapping the flatware piece by piece, taking it from a box by Alyce's chair.

Aaron cleared his throat and looked at her. "I can move to the fort. It won't matter now." There was no point in pretending to be a hapless civilian ship's captain any longer. He could even put on the blue woolen uniform now, for that matter.

"No, please," said Alyce. "Stay here. With you in residence, the soldiers may hesitate to pillage the place. I like to think that if we ... when we come back, there will be something left."

Aaron nodded sadly at the wisdom of this and turned his eyes back to his wrapping. Then he looked up at her again, heartache reflected in his face. "Miss Alyce, if I could stop it—"

"You would still be a Yankee spy. And she would still be a Key West wrecker's daughter," said Alyce. "Besides, I think that if you could stop it, you would have done so before now."

Aaron's eyes dropped back to his work. He did not look up again. "If you ever make your way to Charleston," he said, "I hope you'll take the opportunity to call on my mother."

Alyce stopped her work to look at him with some tenderness. For a second he was just a homesick boy, like her own Richard, God save him. Aaron's mother must surely long for some word from him, even as Alyce pined for news of her own son. "And may I give her your regards?"

"If you please, ma'am." It was his first step toward bridging the gap between himself and his estranged family.

Alyce smiled at his changing attitude toward his parents. She went back to work. "It will be my very great pleasure," she said.

...

At dusk on the Caribbean Sea, the U.S. Navy Caribbean fleet's flagship sailed westward toward the setting sun, its flotilla trailing in its wake. On the deck of the ship, the ensign was at the helm, and the executive officer watched the southern horizon with a worried expression.

The commander, crossing the deck, stopped to mock the executive officer's concerned expression. Then the commander laughed, gave a reassuring pat on the X.O.'s shoulder, and went on about his business.

On a mountaintop east of Havana, a Rebel soldier spotted the U.S. Navy ships in the distance and used the last rays of sunlight to send a mirror signal westward.

The Confederate commander and executive officer, on the whitewashed deck of the Confederate flagship, reacted to the signal's flash from the eastern hilltop.

"That's it! They're on their way. Weigh anchor!"

"Aye, sir ... Weigh anchor!"

A cheer went up from the Rebel sailors on deck, and they moved to get under way.

Well after dark, inside a Tift's Wharf warehouse, Joseph Porter, Josephine Thibodeaux, Bogy Sands, and five other Conch boys hunkered down between heaps of crates by the sickly flicker of a sailor's lantern.

Bogy said, "And I say we can't just leave it all behind for the stinking mudsills to get fat off of."

Porter said, "He's right. Scorched earth. It's the only way."

Joe said, "No! My father and my brother risked their lives to save what's in these warehouses. So did yours. And yours. Bogy, your uncle drowned on Pelican Reef, remember? The cargo he died to save is right here somewhere. It would be sacrilege to burn it down out of pure spite! Won't change a thing."

Porter said, "She's right. Won't change a thing."

Bogy gave Porter a look that caused Porter to shrink a little. Then Bogy jammed a thumb toward the warehouse door, and Porter obediently moved to take up his old position as lookout.

Bogy scooted closer so as to speak directly into Joe's face. "All right. Not the warehouses. But our own houses, then. If we can't live in 'em, the mudsills can't either!"

CHAPTER 14

A murmur went through the group. Joe was the only female present, but she refused to be intimidated. "Whose side are you on, Bogy Sands? Bartlum's house was floated here all the way from Green Turtle Cay, board by board. Roberts' was, too. And the rest have withstood hail, hurricane, and high water. I would kill any Yankee soldier who tried to set fire to 'em, and I ain't gonna stand by and let *you* do it."

In a subtle way, all the boys pulled away from Joe, leaving her to face them alone. Bogy Sands seemed to speak for all of them: "Well, I swear. I'm glad Richard ain't here, Joe Thibodeaux, to see what a Yank lover you turned into."

Joe looked at each boy in turn, and each returned her look with nothing but distaste in his eyes. Only Porter seemed to feel regret, but he stuck with the menfolk on this one.

Josephine Marie lifted her chin, contempt in every line of her body, and backed away from the light into the dark recesses of the warehouse. Silence. Then the creak and whump of a door. She was gone.

An hour later, on Boca Chica beach, a female figure, its skirts tucked into its belt like pantaloons, tossed a branch onto a bonfire blazing before it, then backed away into the darkness. Pine pitch in the fire popped and sizzled.

On the tin roof of a three-story wooden house, behind the wooden railing of a widow's walk, Joe Thibodeaux stood blown by the wind, scanning the southern horizon with a spyglass.

Aaron Matthews climbed the stairs behind her to join her in her aerie. "I need to talk to you," he said.

She turned to face him, the spyglass dangling in one hand. Her posture said there was nothing she wanted to discuss with this man. "About what?" she asked without interest.

"About these." He held out his hand to display the gemstones retrieved from Curry's transaction with Noah Lewis. The stones used by a Confederate spy to pay for services rendered. "I wondered if you might have any more."

Joe glanced at the stones, registered nothing, and turned her back to him. She began scanning the horizon with the spyglass, west to east. "I don't know what you're talking about, but it doesn't matter. I'll be gone in the morning."

"Will you?" he asked. He didn't say *not if I arrest*

you for espionage.

"You know very well—" She stopped; she had seen something. "I knew it! Look!" She thrust the spyglass at Aaron, gesturing toward the east. She pushed him toward the railing, and he raised the glass to his eye, confused.

"Look at what? Where?" he said.

Joe pointed and nudged him in the right direction. "There! See it? He's done it again. On Boca Chica."

Aaron zeroed in on it with the glass. "A false light!"

Joe was already heading for the stairs. "Come on!" she called over her shoulder.

"But I thought you—"

Joe was already halfway down the stairs. "Come on, Aaron!"

He dropped the spyglass and followed her.

Aboard the Union flagship, the Yankee commanding officer stepped up to the ensign at the helm and peered over his shoulder into the darkness. The ship was without running lights.

"How goes it, Ensign? Keeping us out of the shallows?" asked the C.O.

"Aye, aye, sir. We're out of the woods now. I just spotted the Key West light."

On the Confederate flagship, the commander was joined at the forward deck rail by the executive officer.

"Anything yet, sir?"

"They're sneaking around out there in the dark. Probably won't be able to see them until they're right on top of the light—then we should get a pretty good silhouette to shoot at. Let's take in some sail, though. I don't want to run over them in the dark."

"Aye, sir." The X.O. moved away to execute the order.

Joe and Aaron leapt from the small boat they had rowed eastward, from Key West across Boca Chica Channel to Boca Chica Key. They were both young, strong, experienced seafarers and covered the three miles in about half an hour.

They grounded their skiff within sight of the fire, leaped out and slogged through ankle-deep water to the sand. They ran up a strip of beach. Aaron stopped, panting, staring at the bonfire burning red-gold on the shore. Joe ran past the fire toward the water.

"What are you doing?" Aaron called.

Joe scooped up a double handful of wet sand and ran to throw it on the fire then started back toward the water. "Putting it out! Come on!"

Aaron moved to imitate her, throwing wet sand onto the fire. "What's going on here?" he asked.

"Somebody's trying to trick a ship onto Pelican Reef, just like you got tricked in the *St. Gertrude.*"

Aaron caught on immediately. "And they know the Federal Navy is on its way to Key West to help with the evacuation!" he said.

"Is that who's out there?" Joe asked, without pausing in her fire-dousing efforts.

Aaron dropped his armload of wet sand on the fire and stared at Joe. "You mean you didn't know?"

Another voice joined them from the darkness. "No, she didn't, Mister *Matheson.* But I did."

The bonfire sputtered and nearly went out completely.

Aboard the Union flagship, the ensign at the helm blinked at the black horizon in front of him. "Captain!" he shouted. "Captain, sir!"

The bonfire was a charred mess of sand and embers glowing like the red eyes of Florida panthers. A six-foot palm frond, tossed by unseen hands, crashed into the center of the pile, and flames began to lick at it, growing bigger and stronger.

Lila Dauthier stood at the edge of the jungle with her skirt tucked into her belt like pantaloons and a LeMat grapeshot revolver trained on Aaron and Joe while they rebuilt her fire. "Very good, Mister Matheson. A few more like that one, if you please."

"You know, Miss Dauthier, I am impressed," said Aaron while he worked. "You had me fooled from the beginning, but that LeMat doesn't lie."

"Le-what?" said Joe, working, too.

Aaron noted with a spark of hope that the five-pound revolver wobbled slightly in Lila's hand. "Kinda heavy weapon for a woman, isn't it? I figured you for a derringer sort of gal, Miss Dauthier."

Lila placed her left hand beneath her right, stabilizing the weapon. "Yes, but a derringer wouldn't be loaded with buckshot, the spread of which will more than make up for any inaccuracy or unsteadiness on my part." She smiled, and Joe thought suddenly of hungry alligators.

"And please,'Miss Dauthier' indeed," crooned Lila. "Aaron, my darling, I liked it so much better when you called me 'Lila.' 'Lila, my dove,' you used to say, and I thought we were two of a kind. Didn't you get my letter?"

Aaron delved behind his belt buckle and produced the transcript he had prepared in Morgan's office. "This letter?" he tossed it into the fire, which was growing larger and larger. "I got it," he said.

On the Union flagship, the commanding officer came to stand beside the ensign at the helm in response to his summons. "What is it, Ensign?"

"Nothing, sir. I thought for a minute I'd lost the Key West light, but it's fine now. Just a cloud, probably."

The bonfire loomed large and effective on the beach. Aaron and Joe stood together, tired and dirty, watching it helplessly. Lila stood over twenty feet beyond the fire, out of their reach, with the LeMat carefully trained upon them.

Lila referred to the rebuilt fire, "That's going very nicely," then said to Aaron, "Now, before you think to do something gallant but silly, I'll take that pistol beneath your coat."

Joe looked at him, amazed. He looked at her, apologetic, and carefully removed his Army Colt—which he flung into the soft sand at Lila's feet.

Joe looked at the sea and at the fire. She seemed to sniff the air and take stock of the sky and the breeze. She came to an undeniable conclusion and turned toward Lila. "There *are* ships out there! Right now! You can't do this. People might die!"

Lila brandished the LeMat for emphasis. "Don't come any closer, wrecker's brat."

Aaron, now knowing Lila to be Noah Lewis's killer, reached out to stop Joe, who was compelled forward by her deep revulsion. "Joe, don't—" he begged.

Joe was focused solely on Lila. "I don't care who you are or what you think you're doing, this is murder. You can't do this."

"It won't be the first time," said Lila, and she fired.

CHAPTER 15

Joe spun with the impact and fell, bleeding, to the sand. Aaron rushed to her.

"No!" he shouted. Frantic, he removed his coat and folded it beneath her head. He stripped the buttons from his shirt as he tore it off and ripped it into bandaging strips.

His back was to Lila, and his muscular torso formed a wall between Lila and Joe, but Lila was not interested. She was watching the reef, listening for the sound of a wreck.

Joe's right arm and shoulder were drenched in blood but as Aaron stanched the wound, he reacted to her left hand brushing his cheek.

He looked down into her eyes. She winked at him. Her fingers covered his mouth to stop his exclamation before he uttered it.

"My boot," she mouthed without sound.

"What?" he whispered.

"Knife. In my boot."

Aaron smiled. "I love you," he mouthed.

Joe closed her eyes.

On the Confederate flagship, the commander and executive officer, glued to the deck rail, stared forward into the blackness. The Rebel commander reacted and pointed toward the shoreline, where the superstructure of the U.S. Navy flagship was a shadow across the glow of Lila's distant bonfire.

"There they are! Prepare to fire!"

On the Union flagship, the helmsman looked skeptical. The Yankee commanding officer was standing at his elbow, looking far astern.

The ensign said, "There's something funny about that light, sir."

The commander spun around, alarmed. "What!"

Lila was only obliquely aware of Aaron's form stooped over Joe's body. Instead, she watched the sea, her LeMat still in her hand and one foot over Aaron's Army Colt in the sand. "Because I like you so much, Aaron, I'm going to let you live to see your Navy trapped on the reef just like I trapped you—with the help of the late Noah Lewis, of course. So then you won't feel so bad. It should be a spectacular sight, too. 'The bombs bursting in air,' just like that ridiculous song."

Aaron eased one hand toward Joe's boot while Lila mused.

"I do love a good fire, don't you?" Lila said. "I even suggested to that cute little Bogy fellow that the locals should burn the town tonight—except the Geiger house, of course. I am partial to that one for myself. I had hoped to persuade you to share it with me, but ...."

She turned to look at Aaron just as he reached into Joe's boot for the knife. Lila pointed the LeMat at him, suspicious. "What on earth are you—?"

In one swift movement he drew the knife and flashed it through the air.

Lila's eyes widened in surprise. Aaron remained motionless, his hand outstretched from the throw.

"Aaron—" Lila began. The LeMat fell into the sand. Blood dripped heavily beside it. Blood dropped on Lila's feet, on her skirt, and it spread crimson across her chest, where the knife hilt protruded. Lila teetered a second more then fell.

Aaron raced past her to scoop wet sand from the shoreline. He turned back to the fire and found Joe, standing over Lila's body, holding his jacket out to him in her left hand.

"You best wet this and beat it out," Joe said, if a little weakly. "It's faster."

Aboard the Union flagship, the light ahead flickered and grew dimmer. It flickered again, dimmed still more. The helmsman couldn't believe his eyes. "Captain!" He shouted. "False light! False light!"

The commanding officer looked shoreward then

looked behind them—where his suspicions lay. "Hard aport! Hard aport!" he ordered.

The helmsman spun the ship's wheel for all he was worth.

On the Confederate flagship, standing by their guns, the Rebel sailors watched the shadows disappear ahead when the light on shore went out. Their target silhouette had vanished.

The Rebel C.O. shouted, "Fire!"

From somewhere on deck the command was echoed, "Fire!" and a cannon boomed and belched flame.

Joe and Aaron, standing over the glowing coals that used to be a bonfire, jerked their heads toward the cannon's noise.

On the Federal ship, sailors raced to man their guns as a cannon ball whistled overhead to crash into the water, raining seawater and bits of coral down upon them.

The ensign was spinning the wheel aport as hard and as fast as he could.

The X.O., in the bow with a lantern, watched the hull of the ship scrape the edge of the coral reef as they pulled away within a hair's breadth of disaster.

The C.O., watching astern, shouted to his crew, "Return fire!"

Somewhere on deck a shout of "Aye, sir!" was followed by the boom and fiery sneeze of a cannon.

A second later the other Federal ships, spread out in a line behind the flagship, also boomed and sent deadly cannon balls soaring.

On the Confederate flagship, masts and spars splintered like the crack of doom, lines fell, seawater sloshed over the rails from near misses, and several crewmen lay bloodied on the whitewashed decks.

The Rebel commanding officer looked at the line of lanterns now indicating the Federal fleet extending in a chain a mile long. He looked behind his own ship at the beating his smaller fleet was taking. The situation was hopeless. "Signal to withdraw! Withdraw!" he ordered.

...

Just before dawn, in the Fort Taylor infirmary, behind a makeshift curtain of sheets, the medical officer put finishing touches on a bandage about Joe's right arm and shoulder. Gently he eased her arm into a sling. "How's that?"

"Good," she said.

Aaron, watching from a few feet away, was skeptical. "You're sure?"

Joe smiled at him. "Cross my heart and hope to die." Then to the medical officer she said, "Thank you."

"You were lucky," he said. "LeMats aren't famous for their accuracy, and the shooter was far enough away from you that the buckshot spread a ways. So instead of a big hole in your heart, you're stuck with a lot of little holes in your arm and shoulder. You'll be a mite sore, but you should heal up nicely barring any infections."

From beyond the curtain they heard Morgan's gruff voice demanding, "Where are they?"

The medical officer grimaced at the sound, gathered his instruments, and made a quick exit just as Morgan's head jutted through a break in the curtain.

Morgan looked at Aaron. "They said you brought her in."

Aaron nodded.

Morgan stepped through the curtain, looking at Joe. "So, this is the one!"

"No, this is the one," Aaron pointed to a cot beyond Joe, where a figure lay under a sheet.

Morgan stepped to the cot and looked under the sheet. He looked as if he would faint, or if not, he might vomit. Shaky on his feet, he managed to walk toward Aaron. Aaron wore his damp, soot-stained jacket over a bare chest. Morgan grabbed Aaron's lapels, "You've gone too far this time! It won't work, Lieutenant. You are crazy if you expect me—if you expect *anyone*—to believe it."

Aaron, disgusted, picked Morgan's hands off his jacket as if they were bloodsucking insects. "Believe it. She paid Noah Lewis to set a fire for her, and when he couldn't do it for her again—because she'd killed him—she set the next fire herself. I saw it."

Morgan raved, "You saw it! *You* saw it! Since when does what *you* say mean anything to anybody?

You're the same thing you claim she was!"

"I might have been once. That ended when she became a murderer," said Aaron.

Behind Morgan, Joe rose from her seat and went to lift the sheet from Lila's face. Joe stopped and pulled her knife from her boot. "Aaron," she said, "the stones you showed me? Would that be what she used to pay Noah Lewis?"

Morgan turned to look at Joe.

Aaron looked at her over Morgan's shoulder. "Yes," Aaron said. "I think so."

"Then she would have more of the same hidden somewhere, wouldn't she? To pay him again? Or somebody like him?"

Morgan insisted, "You're wasting your time, I tell you. Lila never—"

"I searched her clothing," Aaron said.

"You vulgar barbarian!" said Morgan.

Joe, with only her left hand to use, put her knife in her teeth and grabbed the top of Lila's elaborate upswept hairdo. She gestured to Aaron with a sidewise nod of her head.

Aaron pushed past Morgan to take the knife from Joe's mouth.

"Cretin!" Morgan cried. "What do you think you're doing!"

Aaron made a quick swipe of Joe's knife, and a handful of blonde hair came away. Joe extended the blonde fur ball toward Morgan, who backed away in revulsion.

Aaron took it from her when Morgan would not.

He found inside it a tiny silk bag, deftly hidden. He slit the bag with Joe's knife and emptied into his palm a dozen stones like the ones Noah Lewis had spent in Curry's store.

"There's your proof, Morgan," Aaron said. "You've caught your spy. You have nothing to fear from the innocent citizens of this island. Now call off the evacuation."

Pure hatred spilled from Morgan's overflowing eyes. Rage contorted his face. "Go to hell," he hissed.

Aaron pounced on Morgan with an inarticulate roar. The dandified colonel was no match for a *sane* Aaron Matthews, and the man whose hands now clenched about Morgan's throat was preternaturally strengthened by a temporary loss of sanity.

Joe intervened, shouting, "Aaron, no! Aaron, stop it! Stop it!" She forced herself between the two men and, to keep from hurting her, Aaron had to relinquish his hold. Morgan staggered backward, gasping for air. "He's not worth it," Joe insisted, trying to calm Aaron. "He's not worth it."

Aaron wrapped her in his arms like a drowning man takes hold of a life buoy.

Morgan kept a careful distance from them, cleared his throat, and attempted to reclaim his dignity. "I'll order a transport to take Miss Thibodeaux to the wharf."

Aaron's look said he would not accept water from Morgan's hand if he were dying of thirst. "We'll get there on our own," Aaron said.

...

Dawn had come to Tift's Wharf, and with it had come the Yankee ships that would transport six hundred Key Westers to Port Royal. The U.S. Navy flagship and several sister ships lined the wharf, each taking on passengers in a steady stream. The Yankee X.O., his hands full of papers, assisted residents in finding and boarding the ship to which they had been assigned.

For every Conch family dragging itself up a gangway with a few meager carpetbags of belongings there was a friend weeping on the dock—one who was not deemed evacuation material.

Also on the dock, Arnau, Carmen, the cigar rollers, the Cuban milkman, and others from the Cuban quarter watched sadly, occasionally waving to a departing friend.

Cataline Simmons and Lucy Drake, Stepney Austin and young Salina stood among others from the colored quarter of town, stoic before an ironically familiar picture: unwilling people forced aboard crowded ships. Only this time the unwilling travelers were mostly white.

Alyce and Elias Thibodeaux stood at the foot of the gangway leading to the Yankee flagship, watching the streets for any sign of Joe. Alyce had been weeping. Elias supported her and fended off the soldier who urged them to go aboard quickly.

Sergeant Pfeifer and his patrol lounged in the street outside the front gate of the Lowe house. The front door of the house opened, and Mrs. Bianca

Lowe and Captain John Lowe emerged, carrying their bags.

"Atten—hut!"

The patrol came to their feet and formed two lines outside the Lowe house gate. Captain and Mrs. Lowe acknowledged them with a wistful nod and passed between them on their walk to the wharf.

Caroline Lowe came out the front door, kissed a black servant good-bye, and took her own carpetbag from the servant. She closed the door, leaving the servant inside in charge now. Caroline wiped a tear from her eye, turned, and followed her parents out the front walk and through the gate.

As she passed between the two lines of Union soldiers, they gave her a smart salute. When she had passed through, they closed ranks and marched behind her to the wharf, Caroline's honor guard.

On another street, Sandy Cornish pushed a wooden vegetable cart toward Tift's Wharf. In the cart sat Aaron Matthews in his soot-stained, tattered jacket but no shirt, and sleeping against his shoulder was Josephine Marie Thibodeaux. Aaron stared into space, his face the picture of quiet desperation.

After seeing the Lowe family aboard the flagship, Sergeant Pfifer approached Captain and Mrs. Thibodeaux. "You'd best be getting aboard, Captain. They're filling up. You'll have to ride on deck as it is."

Alyce pleaded, "My daughter is still missing, Sergeant!"

"We'll find her, Miss Alyce," the sergeant

assured her.

The captain pulled Alyce toward the ship. "Come, Alyce. We're doing no good here. They'll find her if she is to be found."

Alyce allowed herself to be aided up the gangway.

Sandy's barrow rattled its way through the watching crowed. Captain Geiger stepped out of the crowd to put a reassuring hand on Aaron's shoulder. Aaron thanked him with his eyes.

Sandy pushed the barrow through the crowd and up to the executive officer.

"Family name?" asked the X.O., consulting his papers.

"Thibodeaux," Aaron answered, trying not to wake Joe.

"Over here," said the officer, gesturing to the flagship's gangway.

Sandy pushed the barrow to the foot of the gangway indicated, and Aaron eased himself out then lifted Joe to carry her aboard. Three-quarters asleep, she nestled against him, putting her free hand about his neck.

On the ship, Captain and Mrs. Thibodeaux had arranged their bags in their assigned corner of the deck, which was crowded with the bags and bodies of the Lowe family and others who were last to board.

The crowd parted to let Aaron through with his burden. Alyce rushed to meet him, weeping and touching Joe's bandages. She looked to him for reassurance, and he half-smiled and mouthed, "She's all right."

Captain Thibodeaux thanked Aaron with a fatherly clap on the back and gestured to where the family's baggage had been piled.

Bianca Lowe hastily dug a quilt out of her bag and came to spread it across the Thibodeaux's luggage then stepped back and hugged Alyce.

Aaron knelt and placed Joe, still sleeping, on the quilt. Gently, he removed her arm from around his neck, kissed her softly on the forehead, and stood to turn away.

The Yankee commanding officer came out of the crowd on deck to face Aaron. He looked carefully at Aaron's blackened, mangled jacket. "Looks like you've been putting out fires in that jacket," the officer said. "I believe I owe you a great debt."

Aaron smiled wryly. "You want to thank me? Drop anchor right now and send these people home."

"I'm truly sorry," said the officer, seeming sincere. "That I can not do."

"Then add me to your list," said Aaron.

"I have no authority—" the officer began.

Aaron interrupted, "My brother is in the Confederate Army, my family is well known in Charleston for its Southern sympathies, and I ... have been known to consort with Rebel spies ... once at least. If anyone deserves exile, it's me." It seemed to have slipped his mind that, as an officer in the Union

Army, he could be shot for desertion if he left the island.

Captain Thibodeaux moved quietly behind Aaron while he spoke. Lazily, Thibodeaux leaned against the mast a few feet from Aaron's back.

The Yankee commanding officer argued, "I think I can appreciate your position, but my orders are clear. I must ask you to leave—"

"I'm not leaving this ship!"

Thibodeaux removed a belaying pin from the rack at the base of the mast and stepped closer to Aaron.

The commanding officer told Aaron, "I will not miss the tide, sir. This ship is leaving immediately—and without you!"

"Over my dead bod—"

Thibodeaux whacked Aaron from behind with the belaying pin then handed it to the officer and caught Aaron as he crumpled to the deck.

CHAPTER 16

The Yankee commanding officer moved to the ship's rail and shouted to Pfifer, whose patrol was standing on the wharf. "Sergeant! Some assistance, please!"

Pfifer motioned to two men to follow him, and the three rushed up the gangway onto the ship. There they collected the unconscious, soot-stained man and carried him back to the wharf.

Minutes later, the crowd on the wharf watched the flagship draw up its gangway and begin to ease away from the wharf. Aaron Matthews lay unconscious in Sandy Cornish's vegetable cart, gently dumped there by Pfifer and his men.

Aboard the ship, Bogy Sands and Joseph Porter edged through the crowd on deck to where Alyce Thibodeaux sat watching Joe sleep. Porter nudged Bogy and mouthed, "Go on."

Bogy fumbled in the pocket of his pants and

brought up something, which he handed to Alyce. "When she wakes up, would you give her these?" Bogy asked.

"Matches?" said Alyce.

Porter said, "Just tell her she was ... we were ... we decided not to use them. She'll understand."

The flagship was gaining momentum, moving forward along the waterfront, several yards off shore. Behind it, the other ships were drawing up gangways, preparing to follow. The ships' decks were crammed with people.

On the wharf, in the vegetable cart, Aaron stirred. His eyes opened. He remembered where he was, what was happening, and rolled out of the cart, stumbling toward the wharf's edge. "No!"

It seemed he would stumble right into the water, following the ship, but Pfifer grabbed him. Still Aaron struggled forward, intent on the departing ship.

Two, then three of Pfifer's soldiers jumped in to hold Aaron back. He dragged them with him several feet before they could stop his forward motion. He stood, struggling, in their corporate grasp. "No!" he wailed like a madman. "Josephine Marie! Josephine Marie!"

On the ship, Joe's eyes were closed, but something penetrated her sleep. She turned her head and murmured, "Aaron?"

"Josephine Marie!" came the cry across the water, growing fainter as the ship proceeded.

Joe woke and looked around. Alyce leaned

toward her as if to quiet her, but Captain Thibodeaux reached in to take her one good hand, pull her up, and guide her to the rail. Groggy, she blinked the receding shoreline into focus. "Aaron? Aaron!"

On the wharf, Aaron derived new strength from the sight of her at the ship's rail. He gave Pfifer's patrol a workout, holding him back. "Josephine Marie!"

Pfifer told his exhausted men, "Let him go. He can't do anything now."

The soldiers released Aaron, and he was off like a shot, leaving his shredded jacked in the soldiers' hands. He ran bare-chested along the shoreline, paralleling the moving ship, shouting, "Josephine Marie, will you marry me?"

"Yes!" she shouted.

He narrowly missed a cat, which yowled and bolted as Aaron did a frantic two-step over it. "I never told you my real name!" Aaron yelled.

"I don't care!"

"I'm an officer in the Union Army!"

"I don't care!"

He stumbled over a water barrel, sending it rolling, nearly sprawling full-length himself, but sheer determination kept him up and running. "I'm the black sheep of my family!

"So am I," she shouted.

Incredibly, he began to unbuckle his belt as he ran.

Joe saw this and couldn't imagine what was

happening. "Mister Matthews!" she cried. "You're going to lose your trousers!"

"I got drawers on, don't I?" He had reached the end of the waterfront seawall. He could go no farther. The ship was passing him, pointed toward open sea. With his last ounce of strength he wrenched his initialed belt buckle from the leather strap and threw the buckle at the ship.

The crowd on deck—and the crowd ashore that had followed Aaron as best it could—watched in silence, mesmerized, as the bronze oval arced, end over end, out over the open water. The buckle was falling, but the ship was moving away, away, and it might be too—

Joseph Porter leaned far out from the rail of the ship and caught the buckle. Bogy Sands grabbed his feet before he could fall into the sea.

A murmur of surprise and satisfaction rippled through the watching crowds. Many hands helped Bogy haul Joseph back from the railing with his bronze prize. Porter worked his way along the rail to present the buckle to Joe.

She kissed it and waved it at Aaron. He stood, panting, on the end of the seawall, his heart in his eyes.

Boom! A cannon blast from nowhere split the air. Women screamed. People scrambled for cover. Seawater exploded just ahead of the flagship. Aaron's head jerked seaward, seeking the source of the shot.

Stepney Austin broke from the crowd on the

wharf and scaled the lookout tower like a rabid chimp.

Boom! Another cannon ball whistled through the air. People screamed. People ran. Soldiers drew their sidearms. Sailors raced to man their posts. The sea near the bow of the flagship exploded, raining concussed fish and water on the crowded deck.

In the lookout tower, Stepney Austin had a spyglass pointed in the direction from which the shots had come. He grinned and shouted to wake the dead: "It's Colonel Good! Colonel Good, back from South Carolina! It's Colonel Good!"

Aboard the colonel's ship, every inch of sail was up, and the schooner was making excellent speed. The crew looked as if they had sailed all night. Colonel Good, standing in the bow with a spyglass in his hand, looked like a very determined man. His voice boomed with unquestionable authority across the waves.

"Belay the evacuation order! I repeat, the evacuation order is canceled! Turn those ships around!"

A cheer went up from men of all colors, all uniforms. A cloud of hats was thrown into the air.

Aaron's face lit up. The flagship was ceasing its forward motion. Aaron began removing his boots.

He dropped his boots behind him and dove off the seawall. He began swimming toward the flagship.

On the ship, Joe gave Joseph Porter a happy one-armed hug. William and Euphemie Curry exchanged hugs and handshakes with Elias and

Alyce Thibodeaux.

On Tift's Wharf, Sergeant Pfifer and his patrol tossed their hats and clapped one another on the back. Sandy Cornish lifted little Salina into his vegetable barrow and began to push it away from the wharf, followed by Cataline Simmons and Lucy Drake.

On the ramparts of Fort Zachary Taylor, the cannon pointed seaward. The sentries at their posts watched with interest the activity in the harbor beyond Tift's Wharf.

Some thoughtful person aboard the flagship casually tossed a rope over the side. When a dripping Aaron climbed the rope he was met at the rail with cheers and helping hands. As soon as his feet landed on the deck, the crowd parted and someone gently pushed Josephine Marie forward into his arms.

A few weeks later, the people of Key West presented Colonel T. H. Good of the United States Army a gold-hilted sword engraved, "the Savior of Key West."

EPILOGUE

In all, fifteen men escaped Key West to serve in the Confederate Army. Two, William Sawyer and Charles Berry, gave their lives.

A few years after the war, Doctor Joseph Porter discovered the link between mosquitoes and yellow fever. His house on Caroline Street, built in 1838, is a popular Key West landmark.

William Curry became Florida's first millionaire, famous for his family's solid gold tableware service for 24, manufactured for them by Tiffany's of New York. Curry's son, Milton, built the ornate Curry Mansion at 511 Caroline Street in 1899. The Curry Mansion is now an inn and tourist attraction.

Capt. John Geiger's family lived in his house on Whitehead Street for 120 years. The house is now known as The Audubon House, a popular tourist attraction. Audubon had sketched in Capt. Geiger's garden when visiting Florida in 1832.

Caroline Lowe's flag was found a hundred years later, when the house was renovated to make it into a night club.

Right after the war, Sandy Cornish and Cataline Simmons built the first African-American church, on Whitehead Street, just about two blocks from the 1847 Key West lighthouse.

Asa Tift, a shipper, sometime wrecker, and owner of Tift's wharf and ice house, built a home on Whitehead Street in 1851 out of coral stone quarried on the site. From 1931 to 1939 author Ernest Hemingway lived in the Tift house, and his wife Pauline lived there until Hemingway's death in 1961. It is now the Hemingway Home and Museum.

The turtle industry flourished in Key West from 1849 until the 1970s, when the turtles were designated an endangered species.

At one time, more than three hundred blockade runners were imprisoned in Key West harbor. Through it all, the guns of Fort Zachary Taylor were never fired in anger.

Authorities on both sides agreed that continued occupation of the fort at Key West by Union forces shortened the war by several years.

READ MORE ABOUT KEY WEST

A Civil War History of the 47th Regiment of Pennsylvania Veteran Volunteers, 1st Ed. Lewis G. Schmidt, Allentown, PA, 1986. *Firsthand accounts of the hardships faced by Pennsylvania farmers at war on Key West—from mosquito bites to water rationing to the high price of oranges.*

A Guide to Key West, Compiled by workers of the Writers' Program of the Work Projects Administration in State of Florida, Revised 2nd Ed. Hastings House, New York, 1941.

Brown, Jefferson B., Key West—The Old and the New. Reproduced in 1973 by the Bicentennial Commission of Florida. *Judge Browne, born in 1857, was the son of the U. S. Marshal in Key West. (In 1896 he wrote an article on reaching Key West by railroad for National Geographic.) When he first published his memoirs, in 1912, many Key West Civil War veterans were still living on the island.*

Diaries of William R. Hackley, Esquire, (manuscript available at the Monroe County Public Library, Key West). *Mr. Hackley was an attorney for the U.S. District Court, Key West, from the late 1820's until 1857. He worked for Judge William Marvin (the admiralty judge who presided during and after the Civil War) preparing briefs on the salvage of wrecked ships.*

Florida Territory in 1844, The Diary of Master Edward Clifford Anderson, USN, W. Stanley Poole, Ed., University of Alabama Press, 1977.

Heroines of Dixie: Spring of High Hopes and *Heroines of Dixie: Winter of Desperation,* Katharine M. Jones, Ed. Mockingbird Books, St. Simons Island, GA, 1955. *The Civil War diaries of Southern women.*

Langley, Joan & Wright, *Key West—Images of the Past.* Images of Key West, Inc./Langley Press, Key West, FL 1982. *Marvelous drawings and vintage photographs of the people and places about 19th century Key West.*

Shepard, Birse, *Lore of the Wreckers*. Beacon Press, Boston, 1961. *Includes detailed excerpts from captains' logs and correspondence from rescued voyagers.*

Sherrill, Chris, & Roger Aiello, *Key West—The Last Resort.* Key West Book & Card Company, Key West, FL, c.1987. *Includes walking tour to Caroline Lowe's house, Tift's Ice House on Tift's Wharf (now called Mallory Square), the Geiger home, the Porter home,*

Bartlum's and Roberts' Bahama houses, the Martello Towers, Fort Zachary Taylor and more. It's all still there!

Wells, Sharon, *Forgotten Legacy—Blacks in Nineteenth Century Key West.* The Historic Key West Preservation Board, Key West, FL, 1982. *An assemblage of tax rolls, bills of sale, census reports, Key West newspapers shows us Stepney Austin's purchase of three small houses for $600, Cataline Simmons's personal emancipation by his owner (***ante bellum***), and Simmons's purchase of the 9-year-old child, Salina, among other things.*

ABOUT THE AUTHOR

One of the joys of being a Florida native is the opportunity to visit romantic, historic places like Key West. Iris and her family have spent many happy times on the island, and some of the best times have been spent in the Key West public library, reading the diaries of people who lived on the island in its early years. The American Civil War was a tragedy of unequaled proportions, and it is good to remember that it was endured by people and families, individuals and friends, not merely political factions or geographical regions. Iris Chacon's many-greats-grandfather, who fought in that war, is buried in Pine Level Cemetery, Oxford, Florida.

CONNECT WITH IRIS CHACON

You, dear reader, are the reason we authors spend hour after lonely hour creating stories we hope will lift your spirits or transport you to places you long to be. You are the best friends I've never met, and I would enjoy hearing from you with your comments or questions.

Iris Chacon

Contact me at:
FACEBOOK
TWITTER
GOODREADS.COM
AMAZON.COM
SMASHWORDS.COM
or by e-mail at
IrisChacon137@gmail.com

SAMPLE CHAPTERS OF OTHER IRIS CHACON NOVELS

FINDING MIRANDA

SCHIFFLEBEIN'S FOLLY

DUBY'S DOCTOR

SYLVIE'S COWBOY

FINDING MIRANDA

An invisible (or, at best, forgettable) small-town librarian, Miranda is accustomed to anonymity. Suddenly, two people seem all too aware of who, what, and where she is: one is the hunky blind radio host who lives next door, and the other is a murderer.

Sample Chapter

Seventy-five-year-old Martha Cleary relaxed in her front porch rocker by dawn's misty glow with her coffee at her side, her binoculars hanging from her neck, and her small-caliber rifle in her lap.

Wide, shady verandas were the norm in the tiny community of Minokee. The rustic frame houses crouching beneath the live oak trees were nearly as old as the trees themselves. No one had air conditioning in Minokee. With their Old Florida architectural design—all wide-opening windows and deep, dark porches—the quirky ancient cottages were cool even when it was hot enough to literally fry okra on the sidewalk downtown. If Minokee'd had a sidewalk. Or a downtown.

Next door—and only a few yards away from Martha Cleary's rocking chair—a screen door creaked open and whapped shut. Bernice Funderberg doddered toward her own rocker, blue hair in curlers, pink fuzzy slippers complementing her floral housedress.

"Yer late," Martha said.

"Yeah, when ya hit seventy ever'thing ya gotta do in the bathroom takes a durn sight longer than it yoosta," groused Bernice. "Did I miss 'em?"

"Nah, not yit." Martha lifted her binoculars and peered off down the narrow asphalt road to where it curved into the thick palmetto scrub a half-mile away. A jungle of vines, palmettos, young pines, and broad, moss-draped oaks pressed close alongside the road. Nothing was visible through the tangle of flora and shadow. "They ain't made the turn yit. Prolly got a late start—like you."

"But not fer the same reason, I'll betcha!" Bernice said with a chuckle.

"Bernice, poop jokes is the lowest form of humor. I am appalled at your unladylike references to bodily functions at this hour of the mor-- Get outta there, you sorry varmint!" Martha raised, cocked, and fired her rifle in one smooth, practiced motion. Bushes rustled in the garden bordering her porch.

"Git 'im?" said Bernice, unruffled by the sudden violence. It's just another dawning in semi-quiet little Minokee.

"I didn't wanna hurt 'im, jest wanted 'im outta my summer squashes." Martha set her rifle aside and shook a fist at the bushes. "Find yerself another meal ticket, Bugsy! I don't do all this yard work fer my health, y'know!"

Bernice snorted. "Yes, ya do, ya old biddy. Say, ain't that them?" She pointed toward the far curve of the road.

Martha hoisted her binocs, focused, smiled, and nodded. "Yep. Here they come."

"Shucks," whined Bernice. "Looks like a shirt day."

"Hush up, ya shameless cougar!" said Martha.

Across the narrow street, first one and then another screen door whined as other house-coated, coffee-carrying ladies emerged and took their seats in porch chairs. The new arrivals waved, and Bernice and Martha waved back, smiling.

"Jest in time," Martha said.

In the distance a man and dog loped toward the cottages, gliding along the leaf-shadowed, warm asphalt, with a soft whhp-whhp-whhp as the man's running shoes met the pavement. He wore faded jogging shorts that showed off well-muscled thighs.

A tee shirt stretched across his wide chest and tightly hugged his impressive biceps. His pale beard was trimmed close to his face, which was shaded by the bill of his Marlins baseball cap. He wore sunglasses. His donkey-sized dog wore a bandanna.

The ladies in the porch chairs sighed and sipped their coffee, all eyes devouring the oncoming duo. As he drew nearer, without slowing his pace, the man angled his face with its hidden eyes right and left and acknowledged each lady with a wave. A mellifluous bass voice rumbled from behind his pectorals, "Mornin' Miz Martha, Miz Wyneen, Miz Bernice, Miz Charlotte."

"Mornin' Shep, mornin' Dave," each lady called in turn. They did not wave back.

The running shoes whhp-whhp-whhpped past the ladies and on down the tree-arched road. The porch ladies rose from their chairs and turned to watch the eye-candy-in-a-ball cap move away from them. When Shep and Dave rounded the next corner, out of sight, all four ladies gathered their coffee cups, binoculars, and (in at least one case) weapons. With contented sighs, Martha, Wyneen, Bernice, and Charlotte went back into their respective homes. Even with a shirt, today had been a good day.

~ ~ ~

An hour away from tiny Minokee, the bigger town of Live Oak steamed like broccoli in a microwave: green, limp, wet, hot, and fragrant. Summer was an infant according to the calendar, but the time-and-temperature sign outside the bank said baby had grown up fast. At barely nine in the morning it was already over ninety degrees in the shade.

Of course, no shade existed (and, for the moment, no air conditioning either) inside the cramped local office of the Division of Motor Vehicles. Miranda Ogilvy might have endured the heat better than most, with her skinny physique and sleeveless cotton sundress, but she was sandwiched between a buxom big-haired Hot Mama and a barrel-bellied, sweat-stained Good Ol' Boy. After languishing in the stagnant line of bodies for nearly an hour, Miranda's toes had been crushed by the platform heels of Hot Mama four times. Her heels had been bruised by the sharp-toed cowboy boots of G.O.B. three times. Neither neighbor seemed aware of Miranda, though she was pillowed between them like a slipped disc in a miserable spinal column.

Silently Miranda forgave her heavy-footed line-mates; it wasn't their fault. Nobody ever noticed Miranda.

"Next!" bleated an agent whose red face glistened between lank bangs and wrinkled shirt collar. Hot Mama peeled her backside off the front of Miranda's sundress, lifted her platform heels off Miranda's numb toes, and shuffled to the counter.

Oblivious to Miranda's presence, the crowd of humanity behind her surged forward, led by

G.O.B.'s pointy shit-kickers. Miranda advanced two quick steps to avoid being trampled. Now at the front of the line, she luxuriated in breathing deeply since no one was plastered against her front from toes to sternum.

Two yards down the counter to the right, the previous customer departed, and Miranda leapt like a gazelle into the vacant spot.

"Next!" an empty-eyed public servant bellowed directly into Miranda's face. The woman was shorter and wider than Miranda and actually leaned to look around Miranda for the next victim.

"I'm here," Miranda said with a smile and a timid wave.

The official started and then focused on the front of Miranda's sundress. "How can I help you?"

Miranda pushed an envelope and her driver's license across the counter. "I need to change the address on my license, please."

"You can do that by mail or on-line, y'know." The tone of voice said, *It's lunkheads like you that cause long lines on hellish days like this!*

"I tried," said Miranda sweetly. "They said I need a new picture taken." She eased her driver's license an inch closer to the official, who looked down at it and frowned.

"Where's your face?"

"Right there in that rectangle, see?"

"That's not your face, it's the back of your head! You can't have the back of your head on your driver's license!" She angled her shoulders as if to talk over her shoulder, though she continued shouting directly into Miranda's nose. "Freddie, they can't have the back of their head on their driver's license picture, right?"

The shoulders squared up toward Miranda once more. "You gotta have your face in the picture, honey." Her eyes said, *What are you trying to pull, sister?*

"I know. They tried and tried. That's the best we could get. I'm sorry. I just don't photograph well," said Miranda. *I'm a sincere, law-abiding citizen, really, truly I am, and it's not my fault your air conditioner is broken and it's two hundred degrees in here.*

The squatty official pursed her lips, glared at the driver's license, scowled at Miranda's collarbone—nobody ever looked Miranda in the face—and after several deep breaths said, "You got proof of the new address? Power bill, phone bill, water bill, mail addressed to you?"

"My first power bill," Miranda said, sliding the envelope further across the counter.

The official squinted at the address on the correspondence.

"Minokee? Does anybody still live in Minokee?" Then, over the shoulder again, "Freddie, is folks still livin' in Minokee?" Then, to Miranda, "You really moved to Minokee?"

"Yes, ma'am, I sure did."

"From where?"

"Miami."

A satisfied nod at Miranda's bodice buttons. *Explains a lot*, said the eyes. "Step over there in front of the blue screen," the official ordered.

Miranda wove her way across the room to stand in front of the screen and face the digital camera.

Minutes passed. Miranda's official approached the camera from the other side of the counter, carrying Miranda's papers, then stood looking about the room. "Ogilvy!" she shrieked. "Miriam Ogilvy!"

From three feet in front of the camera Miranda waved and smiled. "Right here. It's Miranda. Miranda Ogilvy."

"Whatever," said the official. "Look right here." She tapped a spot on the front of the camera. With her other hand she swatted at a fly trying to roost on the camera lens.

The fly buzzed straight at Miranda's face, Miranda reacted instinctively, and the result was a high-tech digital photograph of the top of Miranda's head with her two hands flailing above it like moose antlers.

"Crap," said the official when the new license rolled out of the laminator. She showed the moose photo to Miranda.

"It's better than the old one," Miranda said encouragingly.

The harried official looked at the photo and at the melting masses still waiting in the long, long, long line of customers.

"You're right," she said, handing Miranda the new license together with the supporting papers. "Have a nice day."

"Thank—" Miranda almost said.

"Next!" the woman blared as if nobody was standing right in front of her.

I guess nobody is, thought Miranda and murmured a "Thank you" that nobody heard.

End of Sample Chapter
of
FINDING MIRANDA
by
Iris Chacon

SCHIFFLEBEIN'S FOLLY

Lloyd Schifflebein is obsessed with adopting six special needs children. He has been working and planning toward that goal all his life. But it looks like Lloyd will need supernatural help to (1) keep his business going, (2) find a suitable woman to marry, and (3) convince the adoption authorities that Lloyd's not crazy.

This would all be so much easier if his teapot would stop talking!

Prologue and Sample Chapter

In the oldest and most perfect pottery studio in the universe, the walls glowed with ethereal light. The ceiling was high enough to be hidden by clouds. The only flaw in the studio's splendor was its single door, which was narrow, wooden, plain, and scarred. Through that door bustled a peculiar, small person sporting a cocked stovepipe hat. He closed the door and waited politely for the Potter to acknowledge him.

The diminutive visitor looked like a 19th century sidewalk newsboy, or he might have been a taller-than-average leprechaun. Truly, he could be both, either, or neither, as the situation demanded. He was older than he looked by several million years, but he could pass for middle-aged on any planet. His name was Orkney.

Orkney watched in silence as the Potter fashioned a teapot and then its lid. He watched the Potter paint the raw clay and then set the two pieces into a kiln for firing.

A glance at the nearby workbench revealed a freshly painted vase, an urn, some candelabra, cups, saucers, a platter, but no other teapots.

When a minute had passed, or it may have been a year or a decade (time having no meaning in the studio), the Potter lifted the fired teapot from the kiln and set about painting a face upon it. Orkney neither moved nor spoke during all that time.

"Good to see you, Orkney," said the Potter, at whose smile Orkney nearly floated with happiness.

"You called, Guvnor?" Orkney said, sounding like a London street urchin—which he could be if called upon.

"Time to go to work again, my son," the Potter said, putting the finishing touches on the teapot's facial features. "It's been thirty-two years, seven months, four days, and six hours since the last job, by human reckoning."

"Human. So it's to be earth again, sir?"

The Potter put down his paintbrush and stepped back to evaluate his creation. He produced a neon green card from among the folds of his robe and flipped the card toward Orkney. Orkney remained absolutely still while the card wafted across the room and lodged itself securely in the band of his stovepipe hat. "That's the name and address where you'll deliver this teapot," said the Potter.

Orkney retrieved the card from his hatband and read it. He blew out air. "Coo! This bloke? They think 'e's bonkers already, Guv. This'll get 'im locked up for sure!"

"Just deliver the teapot."

Orkney looked at the teapot with its newly painted face. "But i's still wet!"

A gust of wind swept through the studio, billowing fabrics and rustling small items on the workbench.

"It's dry now," the Potter said. He placed the lid on the teapot then handed the pot to Orkney.

As Orkney accepted the teapot, it grinned and winked at the Potter.

CHAPTER 1: THE DELIVERY

Lloyd had a philosophy: If it ain't broke, don't fix it. If it ain't on clearance (defined as at least 70 percent off), don't buy it. If it's less than 50 years old, it's too good to get rid of. If it's more than 50 years old, it's an antique and therefore too valuable to get rid of. It was a blessing that Lloyd had never married because his philosophy probably would have driven some poor female to commit murder sooner or later.

That's not to say Lloyd was undesirable as a man. Indeed, women above the age of 50 found him adorable and wanted to mother him. Women in their 40s found him polite, attentive, an excellent listener, and the perfect date for weddings, graduations, awards ceremonies, even funerals. Thirty-something ladies felt he wasn't career-driven enough, but he had a respectable investment portfolio and a cute butt. Twenty-somethings at the gym on Lloyd's workout days sent text messages to their friends about his great body—sometimes they even posted Lloyd videos on YouTube.

Despite his positive attributes, however, Lloyd had reached the age of thirty-two years, seven months, four days, and six hours without finding Miss Right and converting her into Mrs. Lloyd Schifflebein. Yes, Schifflebein. A surname decidedly lacking romance in addition to being difficult to spell and way too long a signature for checks and the backs of credit cards.

Supposing Miss Right were willing to overlook the awkward appellation, there was one other impediment to wedded bliss. Lloyd devoted his whole life to his children. Children he didn't yet actually have, but he was working on it. He had been working on it all his life. He had filed his first formal application to adopt on his 20th birthday, having been turned away on his 18th and 19th. This devotion to his as-yet-unadopted children led many people to deduce that Lloyd Schifflebein was crazy. Big and strong, sure. Cute, maybe, but loony nonetheless.

On the afternoon of Orkney's mission to Lloyd's house, Lloyd had laid aside his carpentry tools, locked his woodworking shop, and settled in the kitchen to brew a cup of tea and make an important telephone call. An ancient teakettle on the old Kenmore stove began to bubble and then whistle, blowing steam. Lloyd was lifting the kettle from the burner when his doorbell rang, startling him into dropping the kettle, which shattered into snowflake-size pieces on the tile floor. Lloyd had never seen stainless steel behave that way. It should have been dented or bent, but shattered? And where was the water? How weird.

Lloyd bent to pick up the mess, but the doorbell clanged again. He sighed and stepped over the debris on his way to answer the door.

He opened his front door to find Orkney on his threshold with a brown box in hand, clipboard under one arm, and pencil behind one ear.

"Delivery for Schifflebein," said Orkney. "Sign 'ere, if ya please, Guvnor." Orkney offered Lloyd the clipboard and pencil. Lloyd signed, then he exchanged the clipboard and pencil for Orkney's brown box.

"Well, g'day, Guvnor, and good luck."

Abruptly, thunder boomed out of a clear sky.

Orkney startled and glanced heavenward. He removed his hat respectfully and backed away from the door, keeping one eye on the heavens.

"No! Not luck, sir. I didn't mean luck, sir. I meant to say, uh, Lor' bless ya. G'day and Lor' bless ya, sir."

Lloyd, too, examined the clear skies and even held out his open hand to check for precipitation, but there was none. He turned to thank the strange little man, but Orkney had simply disappeared. Lloyd stepped outside the door and glanced up and down the street, but there was no sign of a delivery truck or driver. More weirdness. What a day. Shaking his head, Lloyd returned to his kitchen with his brown box.

He left the box on the counter, swept up and discarded the remains of his erstwhile teakettle, and walked down the hall to his home office to make his phone call. He opened a four-inch-thick file folder on his desk, found a number, and punched the digits into his phone.

"May I speak with Mrs. Walken, please?" he asked the answering receptionist. "Retired? But she couldn't have been more than 50! ... Oh, really. Well, she sure didn't sound 62. My goodness."

He paged quickly through the thick file and found his answer. "Wow, I guess it has been, goodness, twelve years now that she's been handling my file. ... Schifflebein, yes. You know my case? ... Really! Everybody, huh. ... Well, do you know who's handling my file now that Mrs. Walken has retired? ... Uh-huh. ... Uh-huh. ... Well, would you please ask whoever draws the short straw to call me? ... Yeah, that's still my number. You have an amazing memory. ... Really! Taped to the desk. Goodness. ... Thank you very much, then. I'll wait for your call, her call, or his call, somebody's call. ... Right. 'Bye."

Lloyd put down the phone, slumped in his chair with long legs extended before him. A black-and-white rabbit hopped through the office door, across Lloyd's ankles, and onward to the futon against the opposite office wall.

"Montalban, don't eat my bed," Lloyd said absently. The rabbit reversed course, crossed Lloyd's ankles going the other direction, and left the room.

After several minutes of staring at nothing, Lloyd slapped his knees as if encouraging himself. He rose and returned to the kitchen, where he removed a paring knife from the cutlery drawer and proceeded to open Orkney's brown box. He lifted the brand new teapot and placed it on the stove with its brightly colored face visible from the center of the room. "Goodness, this is providential," he said. "Who sent you?"

The teapot didn't answer, and there was no return address on the brown box. In fact, there was no address at all on the brown box. Lloyd turned the box over and around, but it was blank on all sides. "My goodness," Lloyd murmured.

At the Department of Children and Families, the receptionist delivered a Pepto-pink message slip to the desk of a supervisor. "Walken's nutty guy called," the receptionist said. "Who do I give it to?"

"I'll take it," the supervisor said, and rose from her chair to take the message in hand.

The receptionist returned to her desk, and the supervisor walked down an alley between cubicles to the lair of Hepzibah Stoner, Social Worker Extraordinaire.

Stoner was the unofficial hit-woman of DepChilFam (as she liked to call it, having become accustomed to such amalgamated nomenclature while serving in the United States Marine Corps). Stoner had the compassion of Florence Nightingale, the relentless determination of Indiana Jones, and, sadly, the face and physique of Winston Churchill.

The supervisor leaned into Stoner's cubicle and placed the phone message on the desk. "Kook call," said the supervisor. "Walken strung him along for twelve years hoping he'd give up, but he doesn't get it. Name's Snicklebean, or something like that. Everybody's talked to him at one time or another, but nobody's had the guts to just tell him no and put him out of his misery. Something about the guy seems to turn people soft. Find the file. Go see him. Tell him to get lost, and close the file."

"You got it," said Hepzibah Stoner. "Snicklebean is history."

End of Prologue and Sample Chapter
of
SCHIFFLEBEIN'S FOLLY
by
Iris Chacon

DUBY'S DOCTOR

Doctor Mitchell Oberon leads a quiet life as a single, female orthopedic surgeon, respected in the medical community, but the quiet is gone when a federal agent forces her to take into her home a brain-damaged man who needs to re-learn all the basics of daily life.

Little does she know, he will teach her a few things about the basics of being a single female. That's the good news.

The bad news is, Doctor Oberon and her John Doe are unaware that he was a special undercover agent, and his old enemies are closing in.

Prologue and Sample Chapter

As he fell, he wondered why he had once again

jumped from a perfectly good aircraft. He assumed it was perfectly good because he heard the helicopter's rotor blades beating the air as its engine noise moved off into the distance somewhere above him.

Half-formed thoughts lumbered through his muggy brain.

Pain.

Pain screamed through every nerve ending of his body. So much of it, he couldn't even pinpoint its source.

Cold.

Wind whipped at bare skin as he fell.

Where are my clothes?

Self-preservation bellowed at him from deep within a mind-shrouding fog, *"Look down, Dilbert!"*

He seemed to be stretched out on his back in the air; he fought the up-rushing wind stream to turn his head slightly. In his peripheral vision, Caribbean blue ocean stretched in all directions.

"Prepare to hit the water!" Self-preservation yelled.

He tried to pull himself into a tight ball, rather than smack the surface like a pancake, possibly breaking every bone in his body. If he could become a hydrodynamic object, and if he hit the water at a good angle, and if he could manage to swim or at least float an undetermined number of miles, he just might survive this. *Whatever this was.*

He tried to wrap his arms around his knees and pull them into his chest, but one knee wasn't following instructions. One leg bent toward his torso as he ordered, but the other leg was AWOL for all intents and purposes, being dragged along for the ride. Oh, well, he'd just do the best he could.

Impact was sudden, loud, and painful at a level he had never dreamed possible. He was mildly aware of being warmer now that he was underwater instead of plummeting through air. But the altitude from which he had fallen, combined with his weight concentrated into a small irregular ball, sent him many meters beneath the surface.

Briefly he hung suspended, virtually weightless, in a womb of warm, salty water. He sensed, close at hand, a great darkness that promised relief from the horrible pain if he would only relax and let endless blackness swallow him.

"Up! Up! Air! Air!" shouted Self-preservation.

Leave me alone. I just want to sleep.

"Kick!" Self-preservation insisted. *"Kick your feet! Move your arms! Go up! Up!"*

Reluctantly he forced his limbs to move, though it seemed not all of them obeyed. Still, he followed the bubbles rising from his mouth and nose, and he defied the pain and blackness, until his head broke the water's surface. Involuntary gasps siphoned air into his aching lungs again and again until he was breathing almost normally.

"Float," was the last word Self-preservation uttered.

Lying on his back, the man floated upon the gently rolling sea and let his mind fade into the welcoming darkness.

He neither knew nor cared whether he would

somehow survive the hours and miles of sea that lay between himself and the nearest land.

~ ~ ~

At dawn over Elliot Key, seagulls glided across the pink-blue pastel streaks of sunrise mirrored in the glassy blue-silver ocean. Waves swished against the soft sand that fringed the island, and a sailboat sloughed at its anchor cable. Against the eastern sky, the boat's tri-corn sail formed a romantic silhouette against the sky, while its three-sided shadow doppelganger rippled on the surface of the water.

Halfway between the sailboat and the shore a honeymooning couple rowed their dinghy toward the beach. She giggled at something he said. He crooned something seductive. She laughed and swatted him playfully.

Miami city lights adorned the northwestern horizon like a diamond choker, two dozen miles away as the osprey flew.

Gulls cawed to one another, the sea gurgled against the shore, and the honeymooners' oars softly slapped the water. A breeze off the ocean rustled dry palm fronds. A four-foot-tall blue heron stood sentinel among flying buttresses of mangrove roots.

When they reached the shore, the couple dragged their little boat shushing across the sand onto the beach, beyond the water's grasp. They kissed beneath the rustling palms, and when they stepped apart, the man tickled the woman.

She twisted away, laughing and scolding, and ran from him, come-hither fashion. He pursued. They left two sets of footprints in the dimpled sand as they trotted like children along the beach in the pale dawn.

From time to time the mangrove trees' arching roots crept all the way to the water line, forcing the couple to detour into ankle-deep surf and come back to the sand. At one such spot, the woman was several yards ahead of the man because he had stopped to examine a nearly intact conch shell. She worked her way from sand to water, wading around a mangrove root, and glanced back at her pursuer.

He straightened from his shell collecting and winked at her.

She giggled and turned to look ahead of her again. As she rounded the mangrove, she screamed.

The man reacted to her scream and doubled his pace. He found her standing rigidly beside the mangrove, screaming again and again. He took in the situation and, with protective arms around her, he turned, putting himself between her and the source of her horror: a man's naked body sprawled face down, tangled in the arching tree roots.

A bedside telephone rang at the home of Frank and Mandy Stone. Frank reached across Mandy's impression of Moby Dick in curlers. He lifted the receiver and answered with a sleepy grunt.

"Monitoring per your orders, sir," said a young man. "I think the Coast Guard has your boy out on

Elliot Key."

"Alive?"

"Uncertain, sir. They're airlifting to Jackson Trauma Center."

"Well done. Thanks for the call." Frank replaced the receiver and sank back onto his pillow. He said a short, silent prayer for a miracle, then he rose and began to dress.

Inside a Coast Guard helicopter two medics worked efficiently over an unconscious man. One medic bandaged a head wound while the other splinted and wrapped the man's left leg.

"Femoral artery remained intact. That's the only reason he didn't bleed out. But somebody's got their work cut out rebuilding this leg."

Suddenly the first medic stopped bandaging, felt for a pulse, and swiftly began chest compressions. "May not have to rebuild anything," the medic said. "I've lost him again."

While one rescuer performed cardio-pulmonary resuscitation, the other administered oxygen and verified the intravenous feed was working.

The first medic chanted in time with his rib-crunching thrusts, "*Come* on, man; *work* with me; *pump* for me; *you* can do it."

Minutes later the Coast Guard helicopter landed on the roof of Jackson Memorial Trauma Center. White-coated hospital personnel rushed to the aircraft with a gurney, everyone ducking the still-spinning rotors and resultant dust storm. The two Coast Guard medics helped transfer their patient to the gurney, and one of them followed the team into the building to provide a detailed briefing if necessary.

Such briefings were not often needed now that vital signs and treatment information could be transmitted to the hospital directly from the helicopter, but the personal touch was still appreciated. And occasionally there were questions. Given the circumstances, there were bound to be questions about this unidentified patient, but there would be few, if any, answers.

Frank Stone was not a handsome man on a good day, and this was not a good day. He strode into the trauma center emergency room looking rumpled and sleepy, in a gray polyester suit from Sears. The suit needed cleaning.

He took off his sweaty jacket and revealed his short-sleeved white dress shirt, which he wore with a clip-on bow tie. Shirt buttons strained to cover a beer belly. Frank wore white socks with brown loafers, both nearly covered by the droopy cuffs of slacks that rode beneath his belly, several inches lower than his natural waistline.

No one had ever guessed his age within five years, but people always thought him old enough to know what he was doing.

CHAPTER 1

While not handsome, Frank was winsome in his way. He gave the appearance of a well-used, long-loved teddy bear whose stuffing was lumpy from years of hugging. Nothing about Frank Stone's appearance seemed threatening. When people met him for the first time, his looks were his initial lie, to be followed inevitably by many more.

Stone wove a path through the emergency room's rushing interns, nurses, orderlies, and aides, past a waiting room filled with patients and their families, to the registration desk. There, upon his inquiry, a nurse pointed him toward treatment rooms at the rear, where curtains were drawn around a crowded, noisy cubicle.

A female in surgical scrubs emerged from the curtained cubicle, carrying a chart. Stone nabbed her with a big paw on her elbow.

"Is he talking?" Stone asked.

"Are you family?"

Stone fished a wallet from the pocket of his slouchy pants and showed the woman his federal identification. "Uncle," he said. "Has he said anything? A name? Anything?"

She shook her head. "He's way under."

"You don't know the half of it," said Stone, pocketing his wallet. "How long before I can talk to him?"

She sighed with exhaustion. She had been on duty all night, and this new patient would keep her in the operating room most of the day.

"You'll have to ask the neurology boys that one," she said. "I'm just here to rebuild the leg – mostly the knee – if he makes it. What's his name, 'Uncle'?"

"I can't say."

She sighed again. "Second John Doe we've had since midnight." She nodded to the adjacent cubicle, where no one was working on the patient. "And our average isn't good, so far."

Stone perked up with new interest. "You had another John Doe last night?"

She nodded. Then, in response to a gesture from Stone, the doctor showed him into the dead John Doe's cubicle. A body on a gurney was draped completely. Stone walked to the head of the gurney, lifted the sheet, and looked at the man's ashen, lifeless face.

Then he dropped the sheet, moved to the foot of the gurney, and lifted the covering over the corpse's feet. A toe tag identified the man as "John Doe."

"Whattaya know about this guy?" asked Stone.

"Homeless. Hit and run on I-95 near Biscayne. Looks like he'd been living under the overpass."

Stone snatched the toe tag off the body and shoved it into the doctor's hands.

"For the record, and for the press, I hereby officially identify this *dead* man as Special Agent Yves Dubreau of the Federal Department of Homeland Security. He has obviously been the victim of a freak fishing accident while on annual leave." Stone pointed to the cubicle where multiple professionals were attempting to stabilize the man brought in by Coast Guard helicopter. "*That* one is John Doe. *Comprende?*"

Dr. Mitchell Oberon stared in horror at this scruffy man, whom she liked less with every passing second. Mitchell led the life of a prudish spinster with time for little outside her work; she kept her person and her surroundings clean and tidy. She drove the speed limit exactly, stopped for yellow lights, followed rules to the letter. This sloppy, round, absurdly demanding person wanted her to flout the law. It was almost incomprehensible to her. Speechless, she turned and led Stone out of the dead man's cubicle.

Mitchell took Stone to the admitting desk, where she retrieved the medical chart for the corpse. She shook the chart in Stone's face.

"The answer is no. First of all, that would be lying, and I don't lie. Second, if I did what you're asking me to do, I could be in serious trouble for falsifying medical records," she said.

"Not. *Asking*." Stone spoke barely above a whisper. "Listen very carefully, Doctor: Some very bad people want this guy dead."

He pointed to the cubicle of the injured man. "So, he better be well and truly dead. 'Cause you ain't seen trouble until the bad guys learn he *ain't* dead, and they come in here looking to correct their little oversight."

He picked up a pencil from the admitting desk and tapped the chart belonging to the dead man. "Besides, you won't get in trouble for doing what the law requires you to do. And today I am The Law. Now, mark the chart."

Mitchell glared at the determined man. "Even if the law is willing to overlook it, my conscience will know what I've done is wrong."

He stared at her.

"Let me see that badge again."

He stared at her while he again took out his wallet and flipped it open to reveal his official identification.

Mitchell studied the badge carefully. She was ninety per cent certain it was the real thing. She recalled all the news stories she had read and heard about the nearly limitless power of the DHS. They said even the FBI and CIA had no standing to curb the activities of Homeland Security. She lifted her gaze from the man's badge to his visage.

He stared at her.

As she looked into his face, she felt cold fingers of fear tickling the edges of her mind. Her brow crinkled. "Are you telling me I really don't have a choice?"

He stared at her.

So she took the pencil from him grudgingly and began to erase the name "John Doe" from the dead man's chart. "You'll have to spell that agent's name for me," she said.

On the edge of Coconut Grove loomed an impressive Mediterranean-style mansion with castle-like towers and tile-roofed cupolas. Broken glass studded the top of the stone wall surrounding the estate. All its metal gates were electrified.

A muscular man patrolled inside the wall with a leashed attack dog. As he passed the swimming pool, he waved to the armed sentry who paced in a tower overlooking the pool and tennis court.

Kyle Averell enjoyed an elegant breakfast on a vast teak deck with a view of the courts, where his adult daughter, Carinne, and her coach, Trish, were playing a half-hearted tennis match. Averell looked up when his bodyguard, Rico, emerged from the house with the morning paper.

Rico folded the paper carefully and placed it before his boss, jabbing at a news item with one heavy finger.

Averell put his coffee cup down and picked up the article to read. A moment later he replaced the paper on the table and lifted his coffee cup toward the waiting carafe. As Rico refilled his *jefe*'s cup, Averell commented with mock sentimentality.

"Oh dear, oh dear. A Homeland Security agent killed – while on a fishing vacation, of all things. How ironic to survive vicious terrorists and criminals only to be done in by a trout. Life is cruel."

More sternly, he added: "Carinne will not see the papers today."

"I'll take care of it, Mr. Averell."

Down on the tennis court, Trish was shouting

cheerily at her opponent, attempting to generate enthusiasm. Averell watched them as Rico took the newspaper away. Carinne seemed weary of the game and of life in general. He hoped his daughter would not become the sort of problem her unfortunate mother had been.

End of Prologue and Sample Chapter
of
DUBY'S DOCTOR
by
Iris Chacon

SYLVIE'S COWBOY

Sparks fly – often literally – when a Penthouse Princess is forced to move to the rustic ranch of a Crabby Cowboy. They clash in every way over everything, sometimes hilariously.

It would be funnier, however, if they weren't in danger from unknown murderous thieves.

Will they live long enough to learn to live together?

CHAPTER ONE – THE RANCH

Rural Florida, Outside Clewiston
Two Days Before the Explosion

A dove gray Mercedes Benz limousine bumped along a winding, rutted dirt road through palmetto bushes, spindly pines, and scrub oaks to stop at an open gate with a rusty cattle gap. On a plank above the gate someone had burned "McGurk Ranch" in simple block letters.

Harry Pace, lean, tanned, and dark-haired with silvering temples, slid out of the limo's back seat. He gestured to the driver to stay put, and walked over the cattle gap, through the gate.

Harry had walked farther than any sane person wanted to in the sticky Florida heat when at last he soundlessly approached the front door of the ranch's modest house. He gripped the doorknob. It was locked. He sidled to his left and peered in a window. Nobody inside. From behind the house, he heard someone whistling "Your Cheatin' Heart." Harry smiled to himself and moved in the direction of the music.

In the second-story loft of a hay barn, Walter McGurk was forking hay out the open hay door, sailing it into a battered red pickup truck parked below. The truck's doors were inexplicably yellow. Walt whistled as he worked.

Walt made a heavy job look easy with his strong, athletic build. Sweaty shirt sleeves rolled up to his elbows revealed ropes of muscle undulating in his sun-darkened forearms as he lifted and tossed the hay. His jeans were tight and faded from many washings. His tooled leather belt held a large hunting knife in a weathered cowhide sheath. He wore battered, scuffed cowboy boots.

Harry approached the barn, shielding himself from view beneath a huge avocado tree. When he eased around the tree, a big, ugly dog growled from beneath the red-and-yellow pickup. In the loft overhead, Walt jerked toward the sound and spotted Harry instantly.

"What do you want?" Walt growled, echoing the dog.

"What does any man want when his partners are stealing him blind?" asked Harry, stepping out from beneath the avocado shade.

Walt spun and hurled his pitchfork like a javelin. It thwacked into the ground a hair's breadth from Harry's boots. Only Harry's eyes moved.

"You ain't stupid enough to be talkin' about me," said Walt. "I ain't a thief. Fact, I'm the only half of *this* partnership that ever does an honest day's work. So, what do you want?"

Walt used the hayloft's rope and pulley to swing Tarzan-like to the ground. He paced to the truck, drying his face and wiping perspiration out of his hat with a bandana from his pocket. Walt opened the truck's passenger door and helped himself to water from an Igloo cooler.

Harry walked around the grounded pitchfork to join Walt at the truck. Walt filled a paper cup with water from the Igloo, but when Harry reached for it, Walt offered it instead to the ill-tempered dog lying under the truck. Unperturbed, Harry got his own cup of water. Then he turned his back on Walt and toyed with a heavy avocado drooping from a branch.

"Spit it out, will ya?" said Walt, helping himself to water from the paper cup he had shared with the dog. "Butch and me got things to do."

Harry didn't turn around. "I was gonna ask you to help me when I make my play to get back what they stole," Harry said to the avocado. "But it occurs to me you're probably gettin' too old and too slow."

Behind Harry, Walt bent to reach beneath his jeans and pull a pistol out of an ankle holster.

"I'm twenty years younger than you, old timer, and I can still chop my own guacamole," said Walt.

Harry snapped the avocado from the tree. The branch recoiled, bucking and swinging. Harry feinted one way, then reversed direction, turned, and threw the avocado high. It soared like a miniature green football far over Walt's head.

Walt fired three quick shots, each one chopping a piece off the airborne avocado.

Avocado chunks rained down and littered the grass. Harry walked through them, turning them over with the toe of his boot. Walt slid the pistol back into his own boot. Harry gave him a satisfied nod.

"I want you to take care of Sylvie," Harry said.

Walt shook his head. "I ain't up to spoiling your daughter for ya. You done too well already on that, if ya ask me."

Harry gave him a hard look. "Don't spoil her," he said. "Take care of her."

"You take care of her. Ain't seen her in nearly

ten years. You and I both know she'd be happy if she never saw me again."

"I'll be busy," said Harry. "Gonna give some big city thieves a dose of their own medicine."

"And if they don't want to swallow it?"

Harry turned to leave, speaking almost to himself as he retraced the route to the limo. "Then we'll find out whether *I'm* gettin' too old and too slow."

Butch rose from beneath the truck, and Walt absently rubbed the dog's ears as he watched Harry go. Walt's brow furrowed, and there was both anger and worry in his voice when he shouted, "I got a good life here, Harry. Don't you mess it up for me, y'hear?! Harry?! I mean it, now."

Harry kept walking. He never looked back.

"Shoot!" said Walt in disgust. He splattered a hunk of avocado with a kick and snatched up the pitchfork to return to work. Harry was gone. Whatever would happen, would happen.

A cellular phone rang inside the truck. Walt walked over, leaned in, and plucked the phone from its holster on the dashboard.

"McGurk," he said into the phone. He listened, then responded, "Was that tonight? ... No, no problem. I just forgot is all. ... Clarice, people forget. It don't mean they don't love people. They just forget. I'll pick you up at seven. ... Fine. 'Bye."

He slammed the phone back into its holster and gave Butch an exasperated look. "I think what we need is one more fancy-planning, crazy-talkin', lipstick-wearin' tower of estrogen in our lives right now, don't you?"

"Woof!" said Butch.

CHAPTER TWO – THE OFFICE

Downtown Miami
One Day Before the Explosion

Leslye Larrimore was a 50-ish, elegantly coiffed woman who sported designer business attire and balanced effortlessly on five-inch stiletto heels. Leslye's office at Pace-Larrimore, Incorporated, was an expansive, opulent room with a stunning city view. Mahogany and brass shone everywhere around her as she read her mail at a desk the size of an aircraft carrier.

Harry Pace entered without knocking and sprawled in one of the elegant, upholstered guest chairs across from the desk. Leslye set her mail aside.

"Missed you at Sylvie's last Saturday," she said.

"I doubt if my daughter would agree with you," said Harry. "Surely Dan Stern was there to fill the void."

"Jealous? Harry, really."

"I'm not jealous, Les. I'm her father."

"And he's your business partner," said Leslye. "I

should think you'd be pleased that they like each other. She's not daddy's little girl any longer, Harry. She's going to have other men in her life."

"Fine. Let her have *other* men. Les, can't you get Stern to lay off?"

"You want him to lay off, you tell him. Why are you so against Danny all of a sudden?"

Harry pursed his lips and clinched his fists. He bounced one fist on his knee. "He'll get his tail in a crack someday and do something desperate to get himself out of it. Heck, he may have done it already. I don't want Sylvie to be caught in a crossfire."

Leslye smiled and used her most soothing tones. "I really think you're overreacting," she said. "I don't see any of that happening. Really I don't."

Harry pushed himself up from the chair like a much older man. "I'll pass on dinner tonight, Les, if you don't mind," he told her. "Think I'll go out to the boat and spend the weekend alone. Try to get my perspective back. Chill out. Okay?"

Leslye couldn't quite hide her disappointment, but she tried. "Sure, Harry," she said. "You take care of yourself. It'll all look better Monday morning. I'm sure there's nothing to worry about."

"Yeah, maybe not," said Harry. He left her office, closing the door behind him.

Immediately, Leslye dialed a number on her desk phone. She was irritated when she reached an electronic device instead of a human.

"Stupid machine," she said beneath her breath. Then, into the phone, she said, "Yeah, it's me. Call me at home when you get in, no matter how late."

Then she hung up the phone and chewed at the edges of her expensive manicure.

....

It was 2:45 a.m. by the digital bedside clock when Leslye's cell phone vibrated with a loud clatter on the nightstand and she writhed across silk sheets to answer it.

"Hello," she said, and looked at the clock while listening to the caller. "Well, it's about time. Listen, I think we'd better pay Harry a visit first thing in the morning. This thing could blow up in our faces if we're not careful. Meet me at the marina at nine thirty."

Without giving the other party a chance to argue, Leslye hung up and went back to sleep.

....

Dinner Key Marina, Coconut Grove, Florida
The Day of the Explosion

A silver Bentley pulled in and parked beside the black Jaguar sedan in the yacht basin parking lot. The Jaguar disgorged Leslye Larrimore, who immediately approached a younger man, in Ostrich-skin boots, who angled out of the Bentley.

Attorney Larrimore slung her Louis Vuitton briefcase over her shoulder and extended her hand to the man. He shook her hand perfunctorily before shoving his soft, manicured hands into his pockets, ruining the perfect drape of his linen Euro-style slacks. "Where's Pace? It's hot out here," he said.

Leslye focused her practiced charm at him and assured, "It'll be cooler on the boat."

"It would be cooler in your *office*," he muttered. "This is what I get for kowtowing to Harry Pace. I know you like him, Leslye, but let's face it, Harry is a certifiable kook."

Leslye touched the man's elbow and steered him toward the nearby pier.

"Where are we meeting him?" he asked, scanning the yachts lining both sides of the long, floating pier.

"Out there," Leslye pointed to a sailing vessel moored a hundred yards out into the bay.

"Of course we are," the man sighed.

Together they walked to the end of the central pier, where Leslye flagged down a marina employee in a Zodiac pontoon runabout. In moments the Zodiac had pulled up directly before the couple, and it's pilot helped them board the twelve-foot inflatable.

Leslye negotiated the pier-to-craft transfer with amazing poise even in a pencil skirt and high heels. The man in Ostrich boots removed his suit jacket and loosened his collar; he produced a monogrammed handkerchief and wiped perspiration from his head and face.

"Can we hurry this along, please," he said, commanding rather than asking.

Leslye's smile never faltered. She gestured to the pilot, and the Zodiac putt-putted away from the pier.

Minutes later the runabout, with its company of three, was about halfway between the shore and an out-moored sailing yacht with "Helen" in florid gold lettering on the stern. Leslye delved into her briefcase and lifted her cell phone.

"I'll just let Harry know we're here," she said.

Seconds later, the faint ring of a telephone could be heard coming from the Helen – and a deafening blast vaporized the yacht in a cloud of fire and debris.

Concussion from the explosion rocked the Zodiac. Leslye, her companion, and the marina employee hid their faces from the glaring flames and covered their heads from falling debris. The marina employee shouted "Mister Pace!" and moved as if to dive overboard and attempt a rescue.

Leslye stopped him with a hand on his shoulder, a look, and a wag of her head. Harry Pace, master of the good ship Helen, was no more. Nothing remained but a burning oil slick, black smoke, and floating shards of teak decking.

"You absolutely sure Harry was on that boat?" said the man in Ostrich boots. His voice held amazingly little emotion.

Leslye kept her eyes on the burning, sinking, unrecognizable mass of wood and fiberglas. She nodded.

The man looked back toward his parked car then glanced at his diamond-studded Rolex watch. "Okay. We're done here, then. I need to get back to work."

CHAPTER THREE – THE MORTUARY

Miami—Tuesday Evening
Four Days After the Explosion

Lithgow Funeral Home was an elegant building with white marble columns facing a circular driveway bounded by well-manicured box hedges. It resembled the front entrance at the Academy Awards, with wealthy mourners arriving in their chauffeur-driven gas guzzlers. Everyone who was anyone simply must be seen at the viewing of the late Harry Pace, and they must be seen at their best. The jewelry had come out of the safe deposit boxes for this one. The glittering ladies and their silk-penguin escorts craved cameras, and the local media did not disappoint.

Inside a crowded reception room lined with flowers, sterling candelabra flanked a closed casket. An exquisite oil painting of Harry Pace rested on an easel at one end of the casket. A few of the attendees amused themselves speculating as to how many inches, or ounces, of Harry were actually inside the casket, which must have cost as much as a Space Shuttle.

Sylvie Pace, young, blonde and beautiful (of

course) in a thousand-dollar simple black dress, graciously shook the hands of whatever "mourners" stopped by her chair to pay respects.

Dan Stern sat attentively on Sylvie's right. He was a little older, a lot taller and darker, and a little less beautiful than Sylvie. But Dan always cut a fine figure in his expensive suits and hand-made Ostrich-skin boots.

Together Sylvie and Dan were the South Florida equivalent of royalty, on glorious display.

Leslye Larrimore, looking strained despite her professionally applied makeup, caught Dan's eye from somewhere in the crowd. He gave her a "come hither" gesture. After a few moments of careful maneuvering, Les arrived at Dan's chair. He rose to whisper to her.

"Stay with Sylvie a minute, will you?" said Dan. "I've gotta go outside for a smoke."

"Nasty habit," Leslye told him before taking her seat in the chair he had vacated.

"Yeah, so's Valium," was his snarky reply.

Leslye sent him an overly sweet smile, and Dan headed for the nearest exit.

Walt McGurk's red pickup with yellow doors rolled into the funeral home parking lot just as Dan emerged with an unlit cigarette in his mouth. Dan must have recognized the truck, because Walt stepped out of the driver's side door to find his path blocked by Dan Stern, casually lighting a cigarette.

"Thought you had quit," Walt said. "Smart folks have."

Dan scowled at Walt's black western shirt, black jeans, black Stetson hat, and black boots. "You've got no business here, Dogpatch," said Dan. "Why don't you save Sylvie and the rest of us some embarrassment and just mosey on back to the ranch." He blew a smoke ring directly into Walt's face.

Walt dismissed Dan with a look and walked past him toward the funeral home entrance.

Dan tossed his freshly lit cigarette to the ground and followed. At the door, Dan grabbed Walt's shoulder and pulled him aside. "What are you trying to do!?"

"Just tryin' to pay my respects," said Walt.

"Respect! You and Harry fought like alley cats. Neither one of you ever showed any 'respect' to the other one."

"I didn't come to see Harry. I came to see Sylvie."

Walt shook off Dan's grip and entered the building. Once inside, he worked his way through the throng toward Sylvie's chair. The high-society, glammed-to-the-max crowd scorned his horse-ranch attire with looks and whispered comments. Walt ignored them and presented himself before Sylvie's chair. He removed his hat, took her hand, and pulled her up to walk with him to the closed casket.

They gave no greetings to one another but stood together in silence beside the easel displaying Harry's portrait. Sylvie unconsciously leaned against Walt. When she sniffled, he folded her against him in a brotherly hug.

Gently, Walt told her, "Whatever's in that box, it ain't Harry. Y'hear me? Harry ain't here. You need to remember that."

"I know," replied Sylvie between weepy hiccups. "The preacher said the same thing. I guess Daddy's with Mama now. In heaven."

Walt smiled to himself. "Well, I don't know if I'd give Harry quite that much credit."

Across the room, Dan Stern joined Les Larrimore in watching Walt comfort Sylvie over the casket. Leslye whispered, "I thought you said she hated him."

Dan shrugged. "That's what she says. Avoids him and his place like the plague."

"Well, Danny boy, you better be sure she's had her shots. That plague looks contagious to me," said Leslye.

Dan's expression turned anxious. He moved toward Sylvie and Walt. Coming to Sylvie's side a moment later, Dan gently extricated her from Walt's arms and tenderly ushered her away. "Come sit down, sweetheart," Dan told her. "You look a little woozy."

Dan lovingly helped Sylvie into her chair. Leslye sat in the adjacent seat. Dan said to Sylvie, "Les will get you something to drink." He glanced at the lady lawyer meaningfully. "Right, Les?"

Leslye stood and found herself staring into the shirtfront of Walt McGurk, who had followed Sylvie and Dan. "I'll be right back; you just rest, dear,"

Leslye told Sylvie. Looking up at Walt towering over them, she said, "Good night, Mister McGurk. Thank you for coming." She stepped around him and left in search of a beverage.

Walt scanned the room. Sylvie was surrounded by elegant strangers and watchdogged by Dan Stern. Walt shoved his Stetson onto his head and ambled toward the exit.

Halfway there he stopped, decided he was not leaving, and marched briskly back to Sylvie's chair. He elbowed his way to her and, when Dan refused to yield a place to sit, Walt squatted on the floor in front of her. This put Walt on Sylvie's eye level, and he pinned her with his eyes like a lepidopterist skewers a butterfly.

"Sylvie, you know half of my ranch is yours now. Harry's half," Walt said.

"I guess so."

"Well, if you're in a bind, I'll buy you out fair and square. Cash on the barrelhead."

Dan said, "Really, McGurk! I don't think this is the time—"

"I'm talkin' to Sylvie," Walt said, cutting Dan short.

Sylvie didn't feel like discussing business at all, and certainly not while Walt and Dan were going at each other in front of the jet set. "Can't we discuss this later?" Sylvie said to Walt. "I mean, it's not like I need the money."

Walt's mouth moved as if he would argue with her, but he realized the room had gone silent. The "mourners" all seemed to be staring at him. He stood abruptly, withered the room with a look, and strode for the door.

Leslye arrived with a cup of water for Sylvie. Dan gave Les his chair, and he left to follow Walt, saying to the ladies, "I'll just make sure he finds his way out."

Les urged Sylvie to drink, but Sylvie merely held the cup and watched the door through which Walt and Dan had gone. Leslye patted Sylvie's shoulder and said, "It's all right, darling. Don't let Harry's pet jailbird upset you."

"Harry's what?"

"Jailbird," said Les. "Everybody knows Harry got him out of jail and set him up in that horse-breeding business." Bitterness tainted her voice as she continued, "One of your mother's charity cases, I expect. Harry never learned to tell her no."

Sylvie looked at Les in absolute confusion.

"Honey, they say McGurk killed a man," Les told her. "After all these years, I can't believe you never knew. I thought Harry would've told you all about it."

Stunned, Sylvie gulped the water from the cup like an android. Without looking at Leslye, Sylvie handed her the empty cup. "I guess Harry and I never really talked much," Sylvie said.

Out in the parking lot, Walt was reaching to open the door of his truck when Dan Stern wedged himself between Walt and his goal. "Who do you think you are?" Dan sneered from six inches away.

"Harry's partner, Slick Face. Who do you think you are?" Walt responded.

"Les and I were Harry's partners, Dogpatch. Real partners, in multi-million-dollar joint ventures, not some two-bit horse farm in Podunk Holler. You're not a business partner, you're a joke."

Without raising his voice, Walt responded, "And you're a brass-plated thief."

Dan took a good Ivy League swing at Walt, but Walt sidestepped it and landed a solid back-alley uppercut to Dan's jaw. Dan went down on one knee and stayed there, wiping blood from a split lip.

Standing over Dan with his fists poised for more, Walt said, "Harry never had to worry about finding my hands in his pockets. Tell me, did Harry kill himself when he learned you two had stole him broke, or did you blow him away because he caught you at it?"

"It was a gas leak," Dan insisted, favoring his swollen, bleeding lip. "An accident. Happens every day. You can ask the police, the Marine Patrol, the coroner, anybody." A new gleam entered Dan's eyes, and he smiled wickedly. "But you won't. You don't think I murdered Harry. This," he gestured at the two of them, "is all a smoke screen to hide how you tried to get Harry's half of the ranch from Sylvie before Harry's body was even in the grave. Y'know, if I were going to be suspicious of anybody, Dogpatch, I'd be suspicious of you. We both know you're capable of murder, don't we?"

Walt moved as if he wanted to kick Dan's

perfectly capped teeth down his throat, but he decided against it. He swung into his truck instead.

As the truck roared out of the lot, Dan stood and wiped his face with his Hermes handkerchief. Then he dusted the knees of his trousers and re-entered the funeral home.

END OF SAMPLE CHAPTERS
OF
Sylvie's Cowboy
BY
IRIS CHACON